THE
STOKESLEY
SECRET

Charlotte M. Yonge

1st WORLD
LIBRARY
Literary Society

The Stokesley Secret

Charlotte M. Yonge

© 1st World Library – Literary Society, 2005
PO Box 2211
Fairfield, IA 52556
www.1stworldlibrary.org
First Edition

LCCN: 2004195598

Softcover ISBN: 1-4218-0419-0
Hardcover ISBN: 1-4218-0319-4
eBook ISBN: 1-4218-0519-7

Purchase *"The Stokesley Secret"*
as a traditional bound book at:
www.1stWorldLibrary.org/purchase.asp?ISBN=1-4218-0419-0

1st World Library Literary Society is a nonprofit
organization dedicated to promoting literacy by:

- Creating a free internet library accessible from any
computer worldwide.
- Hosting writing competitions and offering book
publishing scholarships.

The Stokesley Secret
contributed by Tim, Ed & Rodney
in support of
1st World Library Literary Society

CHAPTER I.

"How can a pig pay the rent?"

The question seemed to have been long under consideration, to judge by the manner in which it came out of the pouting lips of that sturdy young five-year-old gentleman, David Merrifield, as he sat on a volume of the great Latin Dictionary to raise him to a level with the tea-table.

Long, however, as it had been considered, it was unheeded on account of one more interesting to the general public assembled round the table.

"I say!" hallooed out a tall lad of twelve holding aloft a slice taken from the dish in the centre of the table, "I say! what do you call this, Mary?"

"Bread and butter, Master Sam," replied rather pettishly the maid who had brought in the big black kettle.

"Bread and butter! I call it bread and scrape!" solemnly said Sam.

"It only has butter in the little holes of it, not at the top, Miss Fosbrook," said, in an odd pleading kind of tone, a stout good-humoured girl of thirteen, with face, hair, and all, a good deal like a nice comfortable apricot in a sunny place, or a good respectable Alderney cow.

"I think it would be better not to grumble, Susan, my dear," replied, in a low voice, a pleasant dark-eyed young lady who was making tea; but the boys at the bottom of the table neither heard nor heeded.

"Mary, Mary, quite contrary," was Sam's cry, in so funny a voice, that Miss Fosbrook could only laugh; "is this bread and scrape the fare for a rising young family of genteel birth?"

"Oh!" with a pathetic grimace, cried the pretty-faced though sandy-haired Henry, the next to him in age, "if our beloved parents knew how their poor deserted infants are treated - "

"A fine large infant you are, Hal!" exclaimed Susan.

"I'm an infant, you're an infant, Miss Fosbrook is an infant - a babby."

"For shame, Hal!" cried the more civilized Sam, clenching his fist.

"No, no, Sam," interposed Miss Fosbrook, laughing, "your brother is quite right; I am as much an infant in the eye of the law as little George."

"There, I said I would!" cried Henry; "didn't I, Sam?"

"Didn't you what?" asked Susan, not in the most elegant English.

"Why, Martin Greville twitted us with having a girl for

a governess," said Henry; "he said it was a shame we should be taken in to think her grown up, when she was not twenty; and I said I would find out, and now I have done it!" he cried triumphantly.

"Everybody is quite welcome to know my age," said Miss Fosbrook, the colour rising in her cheek. "I was nineteen on the last of April; but I had rather you had asked me point blank, Henry, than tried to find out in a sidelong way."

Henry looked a little surly; and Elizabeth, a nice-looking girl, who sat next to him and was nearest in age, said, "Oh! but that would have been so rude, Miss Fosbrook."

"Rude, but honest," said Miss Fosbrook; and Susan's honest eyes twinkled, as much as to say, "I like that;" but she said, "I don't believe Hal meant it."

"I don't care!" said Sam. "Come, Mary, this plate is done - more bread and butter; d'ye hear? not bread and gammon!" and he began the chant, in which six voices joined till it became a roar, pursuing Mary down to the lower regions:-

"Thick butter and thin bread,
Or it shall be thrown at Mary's head;
Thick bread and thin butter,
Is only fit for the ducks in the gutter."

Elizabeth looked appealingly at Miss Fosbrook; but Miss Fosbrook was leaning back in her chair, her handkerchief up to her mouth, in fits of laughing, seeing which, the children bawled louder and louder; and Elizabeth only abstained from stopping her ears because she knew that was the sure way to be held fast, and have it bellowed into them.

Little Annie blundered in her eagerness upon

"Thick bread and thin butter,"

whereupon there was a general outcry. "Nanny likes thick bread and thin butter, let her have it!" and Sam, Henry, and Johnnie directed a whole battery of their remaining crusts towards her cup, which would presently have been upset into her lap but for Miss Fosbrook, who recovered herself, and said gravely, "This must not be, Sam; I shall send you away from the table if you do."

Sam wanted to see whether she would, and threw the crust.

"Sam," she said very decidedly, though there was a quiver in her voice, as if she were frightened.

Sam looked up, and did not move.

"Oh, Miss Fosbrook!" cried Susan, "we were all just as bad. Don't punish Sam!"

"It is time that Sam should show that he has the feelings of a manly boy," said Miss Fosbrook, looking full at him. "He knows that I must keep my word, and that I have no strength to fight with him. - Sam, go and finish your tea on the window-seat."

Her clear brown eyes looked full at him as she spoke, and all the young population watched to see what he would do. He hesitated a moment, then took up his cup

Charlotte M. Yonge

and plate, and sat down in the window-seat.

Miss Fosbrook breathed freely, and she had almost said, "Thank you, Sam," but she did not think this was the time; and collecting herself, she said, "Fun is all very well, and I hope we shall have plenty, but we ought not to let it grow riotous; and I don't think it was of a good sort when it was complaining of the food provided for us."

The children were all rather subdued by what she said; some felt a little cross, and some rather ashamed; and when Mary brought back the dish replenished with slices, no one said a word as to whether the butter were thick or thin. The silence seemed to David a favourable occasion for renewing the great question, "How does a pig pay the rent?"

There was a general giggle, and again Miss Fosbrook was as bad as any: while David, looking affronted, tapped the table with the handle of his spoon, and repeated, "I want to know."

"I'll tell you, Davy man," began Henry, first recovering. "The pig is a very sagacious animal, especially in Hampshire, and so he smells out wherever the bags of money are sown underground, and digs them up with his nose. Then he swings them on his back, and gives a curl of his tail and a wink of his eye, and lays them down just before the landlord's feet; and he's so cunning, that not an inch will he budge till he's got the receipt, with a stamp upon it, on his snout."

"No; now is that a true story?" cried little Annie, who was the only person except David grave enough to speak; while Sam, exploding in the window, called out, "Why, don't you know that's why pigs have rings in their noses?"

> "There was a lady loved a swine;
> 'Honey,' says she,
> I'll give you a silver trough.'
> 'Hunks!' says he,"

continued Hal; "that shows his disinterestedness. Oh, werry sagacious haminals is pigs!"

"For shame, Hal," cried Elizabeth, "to confuse the children with such nonsense."

"Why, don't you think I know how the rent is paid? I've seen Papa on rent-day hundreds of times."

"But the pigs, Hal; did you ever see the pigs?"

"Thousands of times."

"Bringing bags of gold? O Hal! Hal!"

"I want to know," continued David, who had been digesting the startling fact, "how the pig swings the bag on his back? I don't think ours could do it."

"It's a sort made on purpose," said Hal.

"Made on purpose by Mr. Henry Merrifield," said Susan, at last able to speak. "Don't believe one word, David dear; Hal is laughing at you."

"But how does a pig do it?" asked David, returning to the charge.

"Why do you want to know, my dear?" asked Miss Fosbrook.

"Mary's sister said so."

"I know," exclaimed Susan; "Davy went out with the nursery children to-day, and they went to see Mary's sister. Her husband is drowned because he was a sailor; and the Mermaid went to South America; and there are five little tiny children."

"Of the mermaid's?" cried Harry.

"No, no; the Mermaid was the ship, and it was wrecked, and they have noticing to live upon; and she takes in washing, and is such a nice woman. Mamma said we might take them our old winter frocks, and so David went there."

"And she said if she had a pig to pay the rent she should be quite happy," said David. "How could he?"

"I suppose," said Miss Fosbrook, "the pig would live on her garden-stuff, her cabbage-leaves and potato-skins; and that when he was fat she would sell him, and pay the rent with the money. Am I right, Sam? you know I am a Cockney."

"You could not be more right if you were a Hampshire beg," said Sam. "Jack Higgins was her husband's name, and a famous fellow he was; he once rigged a little boat for me."

"And he sailed with Papa once, long ago," added Susan; to which Sam rejoined,

"More fool he to go into the merchant service and get drowned, with nothing for his widow to live upon."

"I say," cried Hal, "why shouldn't we give her a pig?"

"Oh, do!" earnestly exclaimed David.

"I'll catch one," broke from John and Annie at once; "such lots as there are in the yard!"

"You would catch it, I believe," said Sam disdainfully; while Susan explained,

"No; those are Papa's pigs. Purday would not let you give them away."

"Of course," said Henry, "that was only those little geese. I meant to make a subscription among ourselves, and give her the pig; and won't she be surprised!"

"Oh! yes, yes," shouted the children; "let's do it all ourselves!"

"I've got one-and-threepence, and sixpence next Saturday," cried Hal.

"And I've eightpence," quoth Annie.

"And I've a whole shilling," said David.

"I've fourpence," said Johnnie.

"I've not much, I'm afraid," said Susan, feeling in her pocket, with rather black looks.

Charlotte M. Yonge

"Oh!" said Sam, "everybody knows simple Sukey never has a farthing in her pocket by any chance!"

"Yes, but I have, Sam;" and with an air of great triumph, Susan held up three-halfpence, whereat all the party screamed with laughter.

"Well, but Bessie always has lots! She's as rich as a little Jew. Come, Bet, Elizabeth, Elspeth, Betsy, and Bess, what will you give? - what have you got?" - and one hand came on her shoulder, and another on her arm but she shook herself free, and answered rather crossly,

"Don't - I can't - I've got something else to do with my money."

"Oh! you little stingy avaricious crab!" was the outcry beginning; but Miss Fosbrook stopped it before Elizabeth had time to make the angry answer that was rising on her lips.

"No, my dears, you must not tease her. Each of you has a full right to use your own money as you may think best; and it is not right to force gifts in this manner."

"She's a little affected pussy-cat," said Hal, much annoyed; "I know what she wants it for - to buy herself a ridiculous parasol like Ida Greville, when she would see poor Hannah Higgins starving at her feet."

Elizabeth bit her lip, and tossed up her head; the tears were in her eyes, but she made no answer.

"Come, never mind," said Sam; "she's as obstinate as a male when she gets a thing into her head. Let's see what we've got without her. I've only sevenpence: worse luck that I bought ball of string yesterday."

The addition amounted to three shillings and eleven-pence halfpenny: a sum which looked so mighty when spread out, chiefly in coppers, on the window-seat, that Annie and David looked on it as capable of buying any amount of swine; but Sam looked rather blank at it, and gazing up and down, said, "But what does a pig cost?"

"Miss Fosbrook, what does a pig cost?"

Miss Fosbrook shook her head and laughed, saying that she knew much less of pigs than they did; and Susan exclaiming, "There's Purday in the court," they all tumbled to the window, one upon the top of the other.

The window was a large heavily-framed sash, with a deep window-seat, and a narrow ledge within the sill - as if made on purpose, the first for the knees the second for the elbows of the gazers therefrom.

As to the view, it was into a walled kitchen court, some high chestnut and lime trees just looking over the grey roofs of the offices. On the ground lay a big black Newfoundland dog, and a couple of graceful grey-hounds, one of them gnawing a bone, cunningly watched by a keen-looking raven, with his head on one side; while peeping out from the bars of the bottle-rack was the demure face of the sandy cat, on the watch for either bones or sparrows.

A stout, stumpy, shrewd-looking labourer, in a short round frock, high buskins, an old wide-awake, short curly hair, and a very large nose, stood in front of the dairy door, mixing a mess of warm milk for the young calves.

"Purday! Master Purday!" roared nearly the whole young population above; but he was so intent on his mixture, that he went on as if he were deaf, till a second explosion of "Purday! Purday! I say!" made him turn up his face in an odd half-awake kind of manner.

"Purday, what's the price of a pig?" and, "What does a pig cost, Purday?"

"What d'ye all holler at once for? A body can't hear a word," was all the answer they got; whereupon they all started together again, and Purday went on with his mixture as if they had been so many hens cackling.

Then Sam got up his breath again and called alone, "Purday!" and Hal and Susan by pats and pinches strangled the like outcry from Annie and John, so as to leave the field clear for the great question, "Purday, what does a pig cost?"

"More than your voices up there, sir," growled Purday, making some laugh; but Henry cried impatiently,

"Now, Purday, we really do want to know what is the price of pigs."

"They was high last market," began Purday.

"I don't care if they were high or low," said Hal; "I want to know what money they cost."

"Different pigs cost different prices," quoth the oracle, so sententiously, that Miss Fosbrook's shoulders shook with laughing as she stood a little in the background of the eager heap in the window.

"A nice little pig, such as you'd give - "

"Hush, hush, Hal, it's a secret," cried Susan.

"A pretty sort of secret - known to eight already, and bawled out all over the yard," said Sam.

"But don't tell him what it's for; you can ask him without that."

"A nice little young pig," said Sam, "such as you'd keep all the summer, and fat in the winter."

"Mind, it ain't for you, Purday," cried Hal.

"Never fear my being disappointed, sir," said the free-spoken Purday, with a twinkle of his eye, which Hal understood so well that he burst out,

"Ah! you think I can never do what I say I will; but you'll see, Purday, if we don't give a pig to - "

He was screamed at, and pulled into order and silence, ere the words, "Hannah Higgins" had quite come out; and Sam repeated his question.

"Well," said Purday at last, "if pigs was reasonable, you might get a nice little one to fat, at Kattern Hill fair, somewhere about ten shillings, or maybe twelve - sometimes more, sometimes less."

Charlotte M. Yonge

"Ten shillings!" The community stood round and looked at one another at the notion of such an awful sum; but Hal was the first to cast a ray of hope on the gloom. "Kattern Hill fair ain't till Midsummer, and perhaps Grandmamma will send us some money before that. If anybody's birthday was but coming!"

"Better save it out of our allowance," said Sam. "How long is it to the fair?"

Miss Fosbrook's pocket-book declared it to be four weeks.

"Well, then," said Hal, "we three big ones have sixpence a week each, that's six shillings, leaving out stingy Bess, and the little ones threepence, that's three times three is nine, and three times nine is thirty-six, that's three shillings, and six is nine, and very near four is fourteen. We shall do the pig yet."

"Yes, Hal; but if pigs are reasonable, I am afraid three times nine never yet were so much so as to make thirty-six," objected Miss Fosbrook.

Sam whistled.

"Twenty-seven - that's three and twopence - it's all the same," said Hal; then at the scream of the rest, "at least two and threepence. Well, any way there's plenty for piggy-wiggy, and it shall be a jolly secret to delight Hannah Higgins, and surprise Papa and Mamma: hurrah!"

"Yes," said Sam; "but then nobody must have any fines."

"Ay, and Sue must keep her money. That will be a wonder!" shouted Harry.

"Well, I'll try," said Susan. "I'll try not to have a single fine, and I'll not buy a single lump of sugar-candy, for I do want poor Hannah to have her pig."

"And so will we!" cried the younger ones with one voice.

"Only," added Susan, "I must buy Dicky's canary seed."

"And I must have a queen's head to write to Mamma," said Annie.

"Oh! never mind that, such trumpery as your letters are," said Hal. "Mamma could say them by heart before she gets them. What does she care for them?"

Little Annie looked very deplorable.

"Never mind, my dear," said Miss Fosbrook, "mammas always care for little girls' letters, and you are quite right to keep a penny for your stamp for her. - You see, Hal, this scheme will never come to good if you sacrifice other duties to it."

Henry twirled round impatiently.

"Now suppose," said Miss Fosbrook, "that we set up a treasury, and put all in that we can properly afford, and then break it open on the day before the fair, and see how much we have."

"Oh! yes, yes," cried the children in raptures.

Charlotte M. Yonge

"Will you help, Miss Fosbrook?" said Susan, clasping her hands.

"I should like to do a very little, if you will take this silver threepenny; but I do not think it would be right for me to spare one penny more, for all I can afford is very much wanted at home."

"What shall we have for treasury?" said Hal, looking round.

"I know!" cried Susan. "Here, in the baby-house; here's the Toby, let's put it inside him."

The so-called baby-house was an old-fashioned cupboard with glass doors, where certain tender dolls, and other curiosities, playthings too frail to be played with and the like, were ranged in good order, and never taken out except when some one child was unwell, and had to stay in-doors alone.

Toby Fillpot was a present from Nurse Freeman. It was a large mug, representing a man with a red coat, black hat, and white waistcoat, very short legs, and top-boots. The opening of the cup was at the top of his head, and into this was dropped all the silver and pence at present mustered, and computed to be about four shillings.

"And, Miss Fosbrook, you'll not be cross about fines?" said Johnnie, looking coaxing.

"I hope I shall not be cross," she answered; "but I do not engage to let you off any. I think having so good a use to put your money to should make you more careful against forfeiting it."

"Yes," said Johnnie disconsolately.

"Well, I never get fined," cried Hal joyfully.

"Except for running up stairs in dirty shoes," said Sam.

"Oh! there's no dirt now."

"Let me see, what are the fines?" said Miss Fosbrook.

"Here's the list," said Susan; and sighing, she said, "I'm afraid I shall never do it! If Bessie only would help!"

The fines of the Stokesley schoolroom were these for delinquencies - each value a farthing -

> For being dressed later than eight o'clock.
> For hair not properly brushed.
> For coming to lessons later than five minutes after ten.
> For dirty hands.
> For being turned back twice with any lesson.
> For elbows on the table.
> For foolish crying.
> For unnecessary words in lesson-time.
> For running up stairs in wet shoes.
> For leaving things about.

Each of these bits of misbehaviour caused the forfeit of a farthing out of the weekly allowance. Susan looked very gloomy over them; but Hal exclaimed, "Never mind, Susie; we'll do it all without you, never fear!"

"And now," said Sam, "I vote we have some fun in the garden."

Some readers may be disposed to doubt, after this specimen, whether the young Merrifields could be really young ladies and gentlemen; but indeed their birth might make them so; for there had been Squire Merrifields at Stokesley as long as Stokesley had been a parish, and those qualities of honour and good breeding that mark the gentleman had not been wanting to the elder members of the family. The father of these children was a captain in the navy, and till within the last six years the children had lived near Plymouth; but when he inherited the estate they came thither, and David and the two little ones had been born at Stokesley. The property was not large; and as Captain Merrifield was far from rich, it took much management to give all this tribe of boys and girls a good education, as well as plenty of bread and butter, mutton, and apple-pudding. There was very little money left to be spent upon ornament, or upon pleasuring; so they were brought up to the most homely dress suited to their station, and were left entirely to the country enjoyments that spring up of themselves. Company was seldom seen, for Papa and Mamma had little time or means for visiting; and a few morning calls and a little dining out was all they did; which tended to make the young ones more shy and homely, more free and rude, more inclined to love their own ways and despise those of other people, than if they had seen more of the world. They were a happy, healthy set of children, not faulty in essentials, but, it must be confessed, a little wild, rough and uncivil, in spite of the code of fines.

CHAPTER II.

Mrs. Merrifield had taught her children herself, till Samuel and Henry began going to the Curate for a couple of hours every day, to be prepared for school. Lessons were always rather a scramble; so many people coming to speak to her, and so many interruptions from the nursery; and then came a time when Mamma always was tired, and Papa used to come out and scold if the noises grew very loud indeed, and was vexed if the children gave Mamma any trouble of any kind. Next they were told they were to have a governess - a sort of piece of finery which the little savages had always despised - and thereupon came Miss Fosbrook; but before she had been a week in the house Mamma was quite ill and in her bed-room, and Papa looked graver than he had ever done before; and Mr. Braddon, the doctor, came very often: and at last Susan was called into Mamma's room, and it was explained to her that Mamma was thought so ill, that she must go to be under a London doctor, and would be away, she could not tell how long; so that meantime the children must all be left to Miss Fosbrook, with many many injunctions to be good and obedient, for hearing that they were going on well would be poor Mamma's only comfort.

It was three days since Captain and Mrs. Merrifield had gone; and Miss Fosbrook stood at the window, gazing at the bright young green of the horse-chestnut trees, and thinking many various thoughts in the lull that the children had left when they rushed out of doors.

She thought herself quite alone, and stood, sometimes smiling over the odd ways of her charges, and at what they put her in mind of, sometimes gravely thinking whether she had said or done the wisest things for them, or what their mother would have most approved. She was just going to move away from the window, when she saw a little figure curled up on the floor, with her head on the window-seat. "Bessie, my dear, what are you doing here? Why are not you gone out?"

"I don't want to go out."

"I thought they were to have a great game at whoop-hide."

"I don't like whoop-hide. Johnnie pulls the clothes off my back."

"My dear, I hope you are not staying in because they called you those foolish names. It was all in good humour."

"It was not kind," said Elizabeth, her throat swelling. "It was not true."

"Perhaps not; but you did not speak to give your reasons; and who could tell how good they might be?"

"I've a right to my secrets as well as they have," said the little maiden.

Miss Fosbrook looked kindly at her, and she turned wistful eyes on the young governess.

"Miss Fosbrook, will you keep a secret?"

"That I will."

"I want my money to buy some card-board - and some ribbon - and some real true paints. I've got some vermilion, but I want some real good blue. And then I want to make some beautiful bands with ties - like what Papa has for his letters - for all Mamma's letters in her desk. There's a bundle of Papa's when he was gone out to the Crimean War, and that's to have a frigate on it, because of the Calliope - his ship, you know; and there's one bundle of dear Aunt Sarah's - that's to have a rose, because I always think her memory is like the rose in my hymn, you know; and Grandmamma, she's to have - I think perhaps I could copy a bit of the tower of Westminster Abbey out of the print, because one sees it out of her window; and, oh! I thought of so many more, but you see I can't do it without a real good paint-box, and that costs three and sixpence. Now, Miss Fosbrook, is it stingy to wish to do that?"

"Not at all, my dear; but you could not expect the others to understand what they never were told."

"I'd have said something if they had not called me stingy," said Bessie.

"It certainly was rude and hasty; but if we bear such things good-naturedly, they become better; and they were very eager about their own plan."

"Such a disagreeable thing as a pig!" continued Bessie. "If it had been anything nice, I should not have minded so much."

"Yes; but, my dear, you must remember that the pig will be a more useful present than even your pretty contrivances. You cannot call them doing good, as the other will be."

"Then you are like them! You think I ought to spend all my money on a great horrid pig, when Mamma - " and the tears were in the little girl's eyes.

"No, indeed, my dear. I don't think anyone is called on to give their all, and it is very nice and quite right for a little girl to try to make a pretty present to please her mamma. There is plenty of time before you, and I think you will manage to have some share in the very kind action your brothers and sisters are contriving."

Elizabeth had not forgiven, as she should have done, the being called stingy; it rankled on her feelings far more than those who said the word understood; and she presently went on, "If they knew ever so much, they would only laugh at me, and call it all Bessie's nonsense. Miss Fosbrook, please, what is affectation?"

"I believe it is pretending to seem what we are not by nature," said Miss Fosbrook; "putting on manners or feelings that do not come to us of themselves."

"Then I shall tell them they make me affected," exclaimed she. "If I like to be quiet and do things prettily, they teaze me for being affected, and I'm forced to be as plain and blunt as their are, and I don't like it ! I wish I was grown up. I wish I was

Ida Greville!"

"And why, my dear?"

"Because then things might be pretty," said Elizabeth. "Everything is so plain and ugly, and one gets so tired of it! Is it silly to like things to be pretty?"

"No, far from it; that is, if we do not sacrifice better things to prettiness."

Elizabeth looked up with a light in her dark eyes, and said, "Miss Fosbrook, I like you!"

Miss Fosbrook was very much pleased, and kissed her.

She paused a moment, and then said, "Miss Fosbrook, may I ask one question? What is your name? Mamma said it must be Charlotte, because you signed your letter Ch. A. Fosbrook, but your little sister's letter that you showed us began 'My dear Bell.' If it is a secret, indeed I will keep it."

"It is no secret at all," said Miss Fosbrook, laughing. "My name is Christabel Angela."

Elizabeth opened her eyes, and said it by syllables. "Christabel Angela! that's a prettier name than Ida. Does it make you very glad to have it?"

"I like it for some reasons," said Miss Fosbrook, smiling.

"Oh, tell me!" cried Bessie. "Mamma always says we should not be a bit happier if our names were pretty ones; but I don't know, I feel as if one would; only the others like to make things plainer and uglier than they are."

"I never could call your name ugly; it is such a dignified, old, respectable name."

"Yes; but they call me Betty!"

"And they call me Bell, and sometimes Jelly-bag and Currant-jelly," said Miss Fosbrook, laughing and sighing, for she would have liked to have heard those funny names again.

"Then it is no good to you!" exclaimed Elizabeth.

"I don't know that we talk of good in such a matter. I like my name because of the reason it was given to me."

"Oh, why?" eagerly asked the little girl.

"When I was born, my papa was a very young man, and he was very fond of reading poetry."

"Why, I thought your papa was a doctor."

"Well!"

"I thought only ladies, and poets, and idle silly people, cared for poetry."

"They can hardly be silly if they care rightly for real poetry, Bessie," said Miss Fosbrook; "at least, so my papa would say. It has been one of his great helps. Well, in those days he was very fond of a poem about a lady called Christabel, who was so good and sweet, that when evil came near, it could not touch her so as to do her any harm; and so he gave his little daughter her name."

"How very nice!" cried Elizabeth.

"You must not envy me, my dear, for I have been a good deal laughed at for my pretty name, and so has Papa; and I do not think he would have chosen anything so fanciful if he had been a little older."

"Then isn't he - what is it you call it - poetical now?"

"Indeed he is, in a good way;" and as the earnest eyes looked so warmly at her, Christabel Fosbrook could not help making a friend of the little maiden. "He has very little time to read it; for you know he is a parish surgeon in a great parish in London, full of poor people, worse off than you can imagine, and often very ill. He is obliged to be always hard at work in the narrow close streets there, and to see everything sad, and dismal, and disagreeable, that can be found; but, do you know, Bessie, he always looks for the good and beautiful side; he looks at one person's patience, and another person's kindness, and at some little child's love for its mother or sister, that hinders it from being too painful for him."

"But is that poetry? I thought poetry meant verses."

"Verses are generally the best and most suitable way of expressing our feelings about what is good and beautiful; but they are not always poetry, any more than the verses they sang to-night about the bread and butter, because, you know, wanting thick butter was not exactly a beautiful feeling. I think the denying

Charlotte M. Yonge

themselves their little indulgences for the sake of giving the poor woman a pig, is much more poetical, though nobody said a word in verse."

They both laughed; and Elizabeth said, "That wasn't what you meant about your papa. Susy cares for goodness."

"No, it was not all I meant; but it was seeing high and noble thoughts expressed in beautiful verses that gives him pleasure; and when he has a little bit of leisure, it is his great treat to open a book of that sort, and read a little bit to us, and tell us why we like it. He says it makes him young again, and takes him out of the dingy streets, and from all his cares as to how the bills are to be paid."

"Did you like coming here?" was Bessie's home question; and Miss Fosbrook winked away a little moisture, as she said,

"I was glad to be growing a woman, and to be able to help about some of those bills; and then I was glad to come into the beautiful country that Papa has so often told us about."

"I did not know there was anything beautiful here."

"O Bessie, you never lived in London! You can't think how many things are beautiful to me here! I want to be writing about them to Papa and Kate all day long."

"Are they?" said Bessie. "Mamma has pretty things in the drawing-room, but she keeps them out of the way; and everything here is so dull and stupid!" and the little girl gave a yawn.

Miss Fosbrook understood her. The wainscoted room in which they were sitting had been painted of a uniform creamy brown; the chairs were worn; the table was blistered and cracked; the carpet only covered the middle of the room, and was so threadbare, that only a little red showed here and there. All that was needful was there, but of the plainest kind; and where the other children only felt ease and freedom, and were the more contented and happy for the homely good sense of all around them, this little girl felt a want that she scarcely understood, but which made her uncomfortable and discontented, even when she had so much to be thankful for.

Miss Fosbrook moved nearer to the window. Down below there was certainly not much to be seen; only Pierce cleaning the knives in the knife-house, and Martha washing out her pans before the dairy-door; but that was not where she looked. She turned the little half-fretful face upwards. "Look there!" she said; "and talk of seeing nothing pretty!"

"I see nothing -"

"Do you not see the pale clear green of those noble horse-chestnut leaves just sprung into their full summer dress - not in the least worn nor stained yet? And those fine spikes of white blossom, all tending up - up - while the masses of those leaves fall so gracefully down, as if lifting them up, and then falling back to do them honour." Bessie smiled, and her eye lighted up. "And see the colour against the sky - look at the contrast of that bright light green with the blue, so very deep, of the sky - and oh! see that train of little clouds, red with soft sunny light, like a little soft flock of rosy lambs, if there were such things, lying across

Charlotte M. Yonge

the sky. O Bessie! You can't talk of wanting the sight of pretty things while you have that sky."

Bessie was coming closer to her, when in burst Sam and Johnnie.

"Hello, Bess! moping here, I declare! I suppose you and Miss Fosbrook are telling each other all your secrets."

"I was just coming out," said Miss Fosbrook. "I want to make out something about those noble flowers of the horse-chestnut, and why they don't look whiter. Could you gather one for me, Sam?"

Sam was only too glad of an excuse for climbing a tree, however cheaply he might hold one who cared for flowers; and by the time Bessie had put on her lilac-spotted sun-bonnet - a shapeless article it must be confessed, with a huge curtain serving for a tippet, very comfortable, and no trouble at all - he had scrambled into the fork, and brought down a beautiful spire of blossoms, with all the grand leaves hanging round in their magnificent fans.

"What will you do with it?" said the children, standing round.

"Do you think you could ask Mary to spare us a jug, Susan? If I might put it in water in the schoolroom fireplace, it would look fresh and cheerful for Sunday."

"Oh, yes," said Susan, pleased with the commission, "that I will;" and away she ran, while Miss Fosbrook examined the spike to her own great enjoyment. "I see," she said, "the flowers are not really white, they each have a patch of pink or yellow on them, which gives them their softness. Yes; and do you see, Bessie, they are in clusters of three, and each three has one flower with a pink spot, and two with a yellow one."

"That is very curious," said Bessie: the fretfulness was very much gone out of her tone, and she stood looking at the beautiful flower, without a word, till Susan came back, when she began to show her what Miss Fosbrook had pointed out. Susan smiled with her really good nature, and said, "How funny!" but was more intent on telling Miss Fosbrook that she had brought the jug, and then on hauling Elizabeth away to a game at Tom Tittler's ground.

Miss Fosbrook said she would put away the flower and come back again; and she settled the branch in the chimney, where it looked very graceful, and really did enliven the room, and then walked out towards the lawn.

There was a lawn in front of the house, part of which had been formerly levelled for a bowling-green, and was kept clear of shrubs or flower-beds. Beyond was a smooth, rather rapid slope towards a quiet river, beyond which there rose again a beautiful green field, crowned above by a thick wood, ending at the top in some scraggy pine-trees, with scanty dark foliage at the top of their rude russet arms. Fine trees stood out here and there upon the slope of the field; and Captain Merrifield's fine sleeked cows were licking each other, or chewing the cud, under them.

There was a white Chinese bridge, the rails all zigzags, and patterns running this way and that, so that it must have been very ugly and glaring before the white paint

Charlotte M. Yonge

had faded so much.

The house was a respectable old stone building, rather brown and grey, and the stone somewhat disposed to peel off in flakes; the windows large sashes, set in great projecting squared stones, the tallest and biggest at the top. It was a house of a very sober pleasant countenance, that looked as if it had always been used to have a large family in it; and there was a vine, with all its beauteous leaves, trained all across the garden front, making a pleasant green summer-blind over the higher half of the drawing-room windows, that now stood open, telling of the emptiness within.

Christabel stood for a few moments looking round, and thinking what a paradise of green rest this would be to her hard-worked father and anxious mother; and how she should like to see her little brothers and sisters have one free run and roll on that delicious greens-ward, instead of now and then walking to one of the parks as a great holiday. Yet hers was a very happy home, and, except her being absent from it, nothing had befallen her to sadden her merry young spirits; so when she heard the joyous cry behind her -

"I'm on Tommy Tittler's ground,
Picking up gold and silver,"

she turned about, and laughed as she saw the gold-finders stooping and clawing at the grass, with eyes cast round about them for Hal, who was pursuing Susan in and out, up and down till, with screams of exultation, she was safely across the ridge of the bowling-green, that served as "home."

When Hal turned back, Miss Fosbrook was as

heedfully and warily picking up gold and silver as any of the rest of them. He was resolved on capturing her; but first David was such a tempting prize, with his back so very near, and so unconscious, that he must be made prisoner. A catch at the brown-holland blouse - a cry - a shout of laughter, and Davy is led up behind the standard maiden-blush rose, always serving as the prison. And now the tug of war rages round it, he darts here and there within his bounds, holding out his hand to any kind deliverer whose touch may set him free; and all the others run backwards and forwards, trying to circumvent the watchful jailor, Tom Tittler, who, in front of the rose-bush, flies instantly at whoever is only coming near his captive.

Ha! Susan had nearly - all but done it, while Hal was chasing away Annie. No, not she; Hal is back again, and with a shriek away she scours. Sam! oh, he is very near; if that stupid little Davy would only look round, he would be free in another moment; but he only gapes at the pursuit of Susan, and Sam will touch him without his being aware! No - here's Hal back again. Sam's off. What a scamper! Now's the time - here's Miss Fosbrook, lighter-footed than any of the children, softly stealing on tip-toe, while Hal is scaring Johnnie. Her fingers just touch Davy's. "Freed! Freed!" is the cry; and off goes he, pounding for home! but Hal rushes across the path, he intercepts Miss Fosbrook, and, with a shout of triumph - There is the sound of a rent. Everybody stands a little aghast.

"It is only the gathers," says Miss Fosbrook good-humouredly. "I'll tuck them up and sew them in by and by; but really, Hal, you need not pull so furiously; I would have yielded to something short of that."

Charlotte M. Yonge

"Gowns are such stuff!" said Hal, really meaning it for an apology, though it did not sound like one, for her good-natured face abashed him a little.

"Touch and take used to be our rule," said Miss Fosbrook.

Bessie eagerly said that would be the best way, the boys were so rude; but all the rest with one voice cried out that it would be very stupid; and Miss Fosbrook did not press it, but only begged in a droll way that some one would take pity on her; and come to release her; and so alert was she in skipping towards her allies from behind the rose-bush, that Bessie presently succeeded in giving the rescuing touch, and she flew back quick as a bird to the safe territory, dragging Bessie with her, who otherwise would have assuredly been caught; and who, warm with the spirit of the game, felt as if she should have been quite glad to be made prisoner for her dear Christabel's sake.

An hour after, and all the children were in bed. Susan and Annie agreeing that a governess was no such great bother after all; and Elizabeth lying awake to whisper over to herself, "Christabel Angela, Christabel Angela! That's my secret!" in a sort of dream of pleasure that will make most people decide on her being a very silly little girl.

And Christabel Angela herself sat mending her gathers, and thinking over her first week of far greater difficulties than she had contemplated when she had left home with the understanding that she was to be entirely under Mrs. Merrifield's direction. Poor Mrs. Merrifield had said much of regret at leaving her to such a crew of little savages, and she had only tried to set the mother's mind at rest by being cheerful; and though she felt that it was a great undertaking to manage those great boys out of lesson-hours, she knew that when a thing cannot be helped, strength and aid is given to those who seek for it sincerely.

And on the whole, she felt thankful to the children for having behaved even as well as they had done.

CHAPTER III.

"Grant to us, Thy humble servants, that by Thy holy inspiration we may think those things that be good, and by Thy merciful guiding may perform the same," spelt out David with some trouble and difficulty, as he stood by Miss Fosbrook on Sunday morning.

"Miss Fosbrook?"

"Well, my dear."

"Miss Fosbrook?"

Another "Well."

"Is wanting to buy a pig one of the 'things that be good'?'

"Anything kind and right is good, my dear," said Miss Fosbrook, a little vexed at a sort of snorting she heard from the other end of the room.

"Davy thinks the pig is in his Collect," said Sam.

He was one of those who were especially proud of being downright, and in him it often amounted to utter regardlessness of people's feelings, yet not out of ill-nature; and when Susan responded, "Don't teaze Davy

- he can't bear it," he was silent; but the mischief was done; and when Miss Fosbrook went on saying that the wish to help the poor woman was assuredly a good thought, which the little boy might well ask to be aided in fulfilling, David had grown ashamed, and would not listen. But the mention of the pig had set off Master Henry, who was sitting up in the window-seat with Annie, also learning the Collect, and he burst out into descriptions of the weight of money that would be found in Toby, and how he meant to go to the fair with Purday, and help him to choose the pig, and drive it home.

"More likely to hinder," muttered Sam.

"Besides, Papa wouldn't let you," added Bessie; but Hal did not choose to hear, and went on as to how the pig should ran away with Purday, and jump into a stall full of parliament gingerbread (whereat Annie fell into convulsions of laughing), and Hal should be the first to stop it, and jump on its back, and ride out of the fair holding it by the ears; and then they should pop it into the sty unknown to Hannah Higgins, and all lie in wait to hear what would happen; and when it squealed, she would think it the baby crying; but there Susan burst out at the notion of any one thinking a child could scream like a pig, taking it as an affront to all babyhood; and Miss Fosbrook took the opportunity of saying,

"Hadn't you better hatch your chickens before you count them, Henry? If you prevent everyone from learning the Collect, I fear there will be the less hope of Mr. Piggy."

"Oh! we don't have fines on Sundays," said Henry.

"Mamma says that on Sundays naughtiness is not such a trifle that we can be fined for it," said Susan.

"It is not naughtiness we are ever fined for," added Elizabeth: "THAT we are punished and talked to for: but the fines are only for bad habits."

"Oh! I hope I sha'n't have any this week," sighed Susan.

"You may hope," said Sam. "You're sure of them for everything possible except crying."

"Yes, Bessie gets all the crying fines," said Hal; "and I hope she'll have lots, because she won't help the pig."

Bessie started up from her place and rushed out of the room; while Miss Fosbrook indignantly exclaimed,

"Really, boys, I can't think how you can be so ill-natured!"

They looked up as though it were quite a new light to them; and Susan exclaimed,

"Oh, Miss Fosbrook! they don't mean it: Sam and Hal never were ill-natured in their lives."

"I don't know what you call ill-natured," said Miss Fosbrook, "unless it is saying the very things most likely to vex another."

"I don't mean to vex anybody," said Henry, "only we always go on so, and nobody is such a baby as to mind, except Bessie."

And Sam muttered, "One can't be always picking one's words."

"I am not going to argue about it," said Miss Fosbrook; "and it is time to get ready for church. Only I thought manliness was shown in kindness to the weak, and avoiding what can pain them."

She went away; and Susan was the first to exclaim,

"I didn't think she'd have been so cross!"

"Stuff, Sue!" said Sam; "it's not being cross. I like her for having a spirit; but one can't be finikin and mealy-mouthed to suit her London manners. I like the truth."

It would have been well if any one had been by to tell Mr. Samuel that truth of character does not consist in disagreeable and uncalled-for personalities.

Miss Fosbrook did not wonder at little Elizabeth for her discomfort under the rude homeliness of Stokesley, where the children made a bad copy of their father's sailor bluntness, and the difficulties of money matters kept down all indulgences. She knew that Captain Merrifield was as poor a man for an esquire as her father was for a surgeon, and that if he were to give his sons an education fit for their station, he must make his household live plainly in every way; but without thinking them right feelings, she had some pity for little Bessie's weariness and discontent in never seeing anything pretty. The three girls came in dressed for church, in the plainest brown hats, black capes, and drab alpaca frocks, rather long and not very full; not a coloured bow nor handkerchief, not a flounce nor fringe, to relieve them; even their books plain brown.

Bessie looked wistfully at Miss Fosbrook's pretty Church-service, and said she and Susan both had beautiful Prayer-Books, but Mamma said they could not be trusted with them yet - Ida Greville had such a beauty.

Was it the effect of Miss Fosbrook's words, that Sam forbore to teaze Bessie about Ida Greville? - whose name was a very dangerous subject in the schoolroom. Also, he let Bessie take hold of Miss Fosbrook's hand in peace, though in general the least token of affection was scouted by the whole party.

It was a pretty walk to church, over a paddock, where the cows were turned out, and then along a green lane; and the boys had been trained enough in Sunday habits to make them steady and quiet on the way, especially as Henry was romancing about the pig.

By and by Elizabeth gave Miss Fosbrook's hand a sudden pull; and she perceived, in the village street into which they were emerging, a party on the way to church. There were two ladies, one in stately handsome slight mourning, the other more quietly dressed, and two or three boys; but what Elizabeth wanted her to look at was a little girl of nine years old, who was walking beside the lady. Her hat was black chip, edged and tied with rose-coloured ribbon, and adorned with a real bird, with glass eyes, black plumage, except the red crest and wings. She wore a neatly-fitting little fringed black polka, beneath which spread out in fan-like folds her flounced pink muslin, coming a little below her knees, and showing her worked drawers, which soon gave place to her neat stockings and dainty little boots. She held a small white parasol, bordered with pink, and deeply fringed, over her head, and held a gold-clasped Prayer-Book in her hand; and Miss Fosbrook heard a little sigh, which told her that this was the being whom Elizabeth Merrifield thought the happiest in the world. She hoped it was not all for the fine clothes; and Sam muttered,

"What a little figure of fun!"

Martin and Osmond Greville went daily to Mr. Carey's, like Sam and Hal, so the boys ran on to them; and Mrs. Greville, turning round, showed a very pleasant face as she bowed to Miss Fosbrook, and shaking hands with Susan and Elizabeth, asked with much solicitude after their mamma, and how lately they had heard of her.

Susan was too simple and straightforward to be shy, and answered readily, that they had had letters, and Mamma had been sadly tired by the journey, but was better the next day. The little girls shook hands; and Mrs. Greville made a kind of introduction by nodding towards her companion, and murmuring something about "Fraulein Munsterthal;" and Miss Fosbrook found herself walking beside a lady with the least of all bonnets, a profusion of fair hair, and a good-humoured, one-coloured face, no doubt Miss Ida's German governess. She said something about the fine day, and received an answer, but what it was she could not guess, whether German, French, or English, and her own knowledge of the two first languages was better for reading than for speaking; so after an awkward attempt or two, she held her peace and looked at her companions.

Susan and Mrs. Greville seemed to be getting on very well together; but Elizabeth's admiration of Ida seemed to be speechless, for they were walking side by side without a word, perhaps too close to their elders to talk.

Annie and David were going on steadily hand in hand a little way off; and Miss Fosbrook chiefly heard the talk of the boys, who had fallen behind; perhaps her ears were quickened by its personality, for though Sam was saying, "I'll tell you what, she's a famous fellow!" the rejoinder was, "What! do you mean to say that you mind her?"

"Doesn't he?" said Hal's voice; "why, she sent him away from tea last night, just for shying crusts."

"And did he go?" and there was a disagreeable sounding laugh, in which she was sorry that Hal joined.

"Catch the Fraulein serving me so!"

"She never tries!"

"She knows better!"

"I say, Sam, I thought you had more spirit. You'll be sitting up pricking holes in a frill by the time the Captain comes back."

"And Hal will be mincing along with his toes turned out like a dancing-master!" continued an affected voice.

"No such thing!" cried Hal angrily: "I'm not a fellow to be ordered about!"

The Grevilles laughed; and one of them said, "Well, then, why don't you show it? I'd soon send her to the right-about if she tried to interfere with me!"

Miss Fosbrook could bear it no longer; and facing suddenly round, looked the speaker full in the face, and said, "I am very much obliged to you - but you should not speak quite so loud."

The boys shrank back out of countenance; and Sam, who alone had not spoken, looked up into her face with a merry air, as if he were gratified by her spirited way of discomfiting them.

Osmond tried to recover, and muttered, "What a sell!" rather impudently; but they were now near the church-yard, and Mrs. Greville turning round, all was hushed.

Christabel felt much vexed that all this should have happened just before going into church; she felt a good deal ruffled herself, and feared that Bessie's head was filled with nonsense, if Hal's were not with something worse.

The church looked pretty outside, with the old weather-boarded wooden belfry rising above the tiled roof and western gable; and it was neatly kept but not pretty within, the walls all done over with pale buff wash, and the wood-work very clumsy. Sam and Susan behaved well and attentively; but Bessie fidgeted into her mamma's place, and would stand upon a hassock. Miss Fosbrook was much afraid it was to keep in sight of the beautiful bird. Hal yawned; and Johnnie not only fidgeted unbearably himself, but made his sister Annie do the same, till Miss Fosbrook scarcely felt as if she was at church, and made up her mind to tell Johnnie that she should leave him at home with the babies unless he changed his ways. Little David went on most steadily with his Prayer-Book, and scarcely looked off it till the sermon, when he fell asleep.

Miss Fosbrook had one pleasure as she was going home. The children had all gone on some steps before her, chattering eagerly among themselves, when Sam turned back and said abruptly, "Miss Fosbrook, you didn't mind THAT, I hope?"

"What those boys were saying? It depends on you whether you make me mind it."

"I don't mean to make any rows if I can help it," said Sam.

"I am sure I hope you will be able to help it! I don't know what I should do if you did!"

Sam gave an odd smile with his honest face. "Well, you've got a good spirit of your own. It would take something to cow you."

"Pray don't try!"

Sam laughed, and said, "I did promise Papa to be conformable."

"And I was very much obliged to you yesterday evening. The behaviour of the other boys depends so much on you."

"Yes, I know," said Sam; "and I don't mind it so much now I see you can stand up for yourself."

"Besides, what would it be if I had to write to your father that I could not manage such a bear-garden?"

"I'll take care that sha'n't happen," exclaimed Sam. "It would hinder all the good to Mamma! I'll tell you what," he added, after a confidential pause, "if we get beyond you, there's Mr. Carey."

"I thought you did not mean to get beyond me."

Sam looked a little disconcerted, and it struck her that, though he would not say so, he was doubtful whether the Greville influence might not render Henry unmanageable; but he quickly gave it another turn. "Only you must not plague us about London manners."

"I don't know what you mean by London manners. Do you mean not bawling at tea? for I mean to insist upon that, I assure you, and I want you to help me."

"Oh! not being finikin, and mincing, and nonsensical!"

"I hope I'm not so!" said Miss Fosbrook, laughing heartily; "but I'll tell you one thing, Sam, that I do wish you would leave off - and that is teazing. I don't know whether that is country manners, but I don't like to see a sensible kind fellow like you just go out of your way to say something mortifying to a younger one."

"You don't know," said Sam. "It is fun. They like it."

"If they really like it, there is no objection. I know I should like very much to have my brother here quizzing me; but you know very well there are two sorts of such fun, and one that is only sport to the stronger side."

Charlotte M. Yonge

"Bessie is so ridiculous."

"She is the very one I want to protect. I don't think that teazing her does any good; it only gives her cross feelings. And she really has more right on her side than you think. You might be just as honest and bold if you were less rude and bearish."

"I can't bear to see her so affected and perked up."

"It is not affectation. She is really more gentle and quiet than you are; you don't think it so in your Mamma, and she is like her."

"Mamma is not like Bessie."

"And then about Davy. How could you go and stop the poor little boy when he was trying to think and feel rightly?"

"He was so funny," repeated Sam.

"I hope you will think another time whether your fun is safe and kind."

"One can't be so particular," he said impatiently.

"I am sorry to hear it. I thought the only way to do right was to be particular."

He grunted, and flung away from her. She was vexed to have sent him off in such a mood; but, unmannerly as he was, she saw so much good in him, that she could not but hope he would be her friend and ally.

Dinner went off very peaceably , and then Susan

fetched her two darlings from the nursery, George and Sarah, of three years and eighteen months old. Her great perfection was as a motherly elder sister; and even Sam was gentle to these little things, and played with them very nicely.

Miss Fosbrook reminded Hal of his Collect; but he observed that there was plenty of time, and continued to stand by the window, pursuing the flies with his finger, not killing them, but tormenting them and David very seriously, by making them think he would - not a very pretty business for the day when all things should be happy, more like that which is always found "for idle hands to do."

Evening service-time put an end to this sport; but Miss Fosbrook could not set off till after a severe conflict with Johnnie. She had decreed that he should not go again that day, after his behaviour in the morning; and perhaps he would not have minded this punishment much if David had not been going, which made him think it a disgrace. So, in the most independent manner be put on his hat, and was marching off, when Miss Fosbrook stood in front of him, and ordered him back.

He repeated, "I'm going to church." It was plain enough that he had heard what those boys had said about not submitting.

"Church is not the place to go to in a fit of wilfulness, Johnnie," she said; and his sisters broke out, "O Johnnie!" but the naughty boy, fancying, perhaps, that want of time would lead to his getting his own way, marched on, sticking up his toes very high in the air.

Hal laughed.

"Johnnie, Johnnie dear," entreated Susan, "what would Mamma say?"

John would not hear, and walked on.

"John," said Miss Fosbrook, "if you do not come back directly, I must carry you."

She had measured her strength with his: he was only eight years old, and she believed that she could carry him; but he heard the church-bells ringing, and thought he should have his way.

She laid hold of him, and he began fighting and kicking, in stout shoes, whose thumps were no joke. She held fast, but she felt frightened, and doubtful of the issue of the struggle; and again there was Hal laughing.

"For-shame, Henry!" burst out Sam; and the same moment those two feet were secured, and John was a prisoner. Miss Fosbrook called out to the rest to go on to church, and she and Sam dragged the boy up to the nursery, and shut him in there, roaring passionately.

Nurse Freeman, knowing nothing about it, could not believe but that the stranger lady had made her child naughty, and said something about their Mamma letting him go to church; and "when the child wished to go to church, it seemed strange he should not."

Miss Fosbrook would not defend herself, for she was in great haste; but Sam exclaimed, "Stuff! he was as naughty as could be all this morning, and only wanted to go now because he was told not."

Johnnie bellowed out something else, but Miss Fosbrook would not let Sam go on; she touched his arm, and drew him off with her, he exclaiming, "Foolish old Freeman! she will pet and spoil him all church-time, till he is worse than ever."

It was lucky for her that she was too much hurried to dwell on this vexation; she almost ran to save herself from being late, and scarcely heard Sam's mutterings about wishing to break Martin Greville's head.

"You need not hurry so much," he said; "there's a shorter cut, only I suppose you can't get through a gap."

"Can't I?" she laughed; and he led her on straight through the Short-horns. Some of them looked at her more than she fancied, but she knew she might give up all hopes of Sam if he detected her fears. Then came the gap, where a tree had been cut down in the hedge, and such a jump down from it! But she gathered up her muslin, and made her leap so gallantly, that the boy cried,

"Hurrah! well done!" and came and walked close to her, saying confidentially, "I say, do you think we shall ever do the pig?"

"I am sure it might be done. If you are likely to do it you must know better than I."

"I don't know that I much care about it. It will be rather a bother; only now we have said it, I shall hate it if we don't do it."

"I think the pleasure of giving it will be a delightful

reward for a little self-command."

"Only Hal and the girls will make such a work about it. I'm glad, after all, that Bessie has nothing to do with it, or she would want to dress it up in flowers and ribbons. Ha-ha! But what a little crab it is!"

"Don't be too sure of that. People may have other designs."

"Bessie's can't be anything but trumpery."

"Sometimes present trumpery is a step to something better. 'A was an Archer' is not very wise, but it is the road to reading - and even if it were not so, Sam, it is not right to shame people into giving; for what is not bestowed for the true reasons, does no good to giver nor to receiver.

Sam looked up with a frown of attention, as if he were trying to take in the new light; but he did take it in, and smacking his hands together with a noise like a pistol-shot, said, "Ay, that's it! We don't want what is grudged."

Miss Fosbrook thought of words that would another time be more familiar to Sam. "Not grudgingly, nor of necessity, for God loveth a cheerful giver."

What she said was, "You see, if you plague Bessie too much, to make her like ourselves, when she is really so different, you are driving her to the shamming you despise so much."

"But ought not she to be cured of being silly?"

"When we have quite made up our minds upon what silliness is. There, the bell has stopped."

CHAPTER IV.

The most part of church-time Johnnie was eating Nurse Freeman's plum-cake. Perhaps this did not make him any easier in the conscience, but he had a very unlucky sentiment, that as he was already naughty and in disgrace, it was of no use to take the trouble of being good till he could make a fresh beginning; and after what the Grevilles had said, he did not think that would be till Papa and Mamma came home; he did not at all mean to give in to a girl that was not even twenty. So he would not turn to the only wise thing he could have done, the learning of his Collect, but he teased Nurse out of more cake and more, and got what play he could out of little George, and that was not much, for Johnnie was not in a temper to be pleasant with a little one.

Coming home from church, Collects were to be learnt and said before tea: but Hal, after glancing over his own, took up his cap and said, "Come along, Sam, Purday will be feeding the pigs; I want to choose the size of ours."

"I've not done," said Sam.

"Papa never said we were to say them to Miss Fosbrook."

"He meant it though," was all Sam's answer. "Don't

hinder me."

"Well, I've no notion of being bound by what people mean," continued Hal; and no one could imagine the torment he made himself, neither going nor staying, arguing the matter with his elder brother, as if Sam's coming would justify him, and interrupting everyone; till at last Miss Fosbrook gathered all her spirit, and ordered him either to sit down and learn properly at once, or to go quite away. She was very much vexed, for Henry had been the most obliging and good-natured of all at first, and likely to be fond of her; but such a great talker could not fail to be weak, and his vanity had been set against her. He looked saucy at first, and much inclined to resist; if he had seen any sympathy for him in Sam he might have done so, but Miss Fosbrook's steady eye was too much for him, so he saved his dignity, as he thought, by exclaiming, "I'm sure I don't want to stay in this stuffy hole with such a set of owls; I shall go to Purday." And off he marched.

The others stayed, and said their Collects and Catechism very respectably, all but John, who had not learned the Collect at all, and was sent into another room to finish it, to which he made no resistance; he had had enough of actual fighting with Miss Fosbrook.

Then she offered to read a story to the others, but she found that this was distasteful even to her friend Sam; he thought it stupid to be read to, and said he should see after Hal; David trotted after him, and Susan and Anne repaired to the nursery to play with the little ones and the baby. She minded it the less, as they all had some purpose; but she had already been vexed to find that all but Davy preferred the most arrant vacant idleness to anything rational. To be sure, Susan

Charlotte M. Yonge

sometimes, Bessie and Hal always, would read any book that made no pretensions to be instructive, but even a fact about a lion or an elephant made them detect wisdom in disguise, and throw it aside. She thought, however, she would make the most of Bessie, and asked whether she would like to hear reading, or read to herself.

"To myself," said Bessie; and there was a silence, while Miss Fosbrook, glad of the quiet, began reading her Christian Year. Presently she heard a voice so low that it seemed at a distance and it made her start, for it was saying "Christabel!" then she almost laughed, for it seemed to have been an audacious experiment, to judge by little Elizabeth's scared looks and the glow on her cheeks.

"May I say it sometimes when we are alone together?" she said timidly. "I do like it so much!"

"If it is such a pleasure to you, I would not deprive you of it," said Miss Fosbrook, laughing; "but don't do so, except when we are alone, for your Mamma would not like me to seem younger still."

"Oh, thank you! Isn't it a nice secret?" cried Bessie, clinging to her hand: "and will you let me hug you sometimes?"

A little love was pleasant to Miss Fosbrook, when she was feeling lonely, and she took Bessie in her lap, and they exchanged caresses, to the damage of the collar that Miss Fosbrook's sister had worked for her.

"And you don't call me silly?" cried Bessie.

"That depends," was the answer, with some arch fun; but Bessie had not much turn for fun, and presently went on -

"And you saw Ida Greville?"

"Yes."

"What did you think of her?"

"I had not much opportunity of learning what to think."

"But her parasol, and her bird! Did you think her mama very silly to give her pretty things?"

"No, certainly not, unless she wore them at unsuitable times, or thought too much about them."

"Ida has so many, she does not think of them at all. And she has shells, and such a lovely work-box, and picture-books; she has all she wants."

"Are you quite sure?"

"Oh, yes, quite sure! and they don't tease her for liking pretty things; her brothers keep quite away, and never bother about the schoolroom; but she learns Italian and German, and drawing and singing. Mr. Greville said something about our spending the day there. Oh! if we do but go! Won't you, Miss Fosbrook?"

"If I am asked, and if your Mamma would wish it."

"Oh, Mamma always lets us go, except once - when - when -"

"When what?"

"When I cried," said Elizabeth, hanging down her head; "I couldn't help it. It did seem so tiresome here, and she said I was learning to be discontented; but nobody can help wishing, can they?"

"There must be a way of not breaking the Tenth Commandment."

"I don't covet; I don't want to take things away from Ida, only to have the same."

"Yes; but what does the explanation at the end of the Duty to our Neighbour say, filling out that Commandment?"

"I think I'll go and see what Susie is doing," said Elizabeth.

Christabel sighed as the little girl walked off, displeased at having her repinings set before her in a graver light than that in which she had hitherto chosen to regard them.

She saw no more of her charges till tea-time, when the bell brought them from different quarters, Johnnie with such a grimy collar and dirty hands, that he was a very un-Sunday-like figure, and she would have sent him away to make himself decent, but that she was desirous of not over-tormenting him.

Sunday was always celebrated by having treacle with the bread, so the butter riot was happily escaped; and Bessie was not in a gracious mood, and the corners of her mouth provoked the boys to begin on what they knew would make her afford them sport. Hal first: "I say, Bet, didn't Purday want his gun to-day at church?"

Elizabeth put out her lip in expectation that something unpleasant was intended, and other voices were not slow to ask an explanation.

"Shooting the cocky-olly birds!"

A general explosion of laughter.

"I say (always the preface to the boy's wit), shall I get a jay down off the barn to stick into your hat, Betty?"

"Don't, Hal," said such a deplorable offended voice, that Sam, who had really held his tongue at first, could not help chiming in,

"No, no; a cock-sparrow, for her London manners."

"No, that's for me, Sam," said Christabel good-humouredly. "A London-bred sparrow; a pert forward chit."

She really had found a safety-valve; the boys were entertained, and diverted from their attack on their favourite victim, by finding everyone an appropriate bird; and when they came to "Tomtits" and "Dish-washers," were so astonished at Miss Fosbrook's never having seen either, that they instantly fell into the greatest haste to finish their tea, and conduct her into the garden, and through a course of birds, eggs, and nests, about which, as soon as she was assured that there was to be no bird's-nesting, she was very eager.

Bessie ought to have been thankful that her persecutors

were called off, but she was in a dismal mood, and was taken with a fit of displeasure that her own Christabel Angela was following the rabble rout into the garden, instead of staying in the school-room at her service.

The reason of her gloom was, that Miss Fosbrook had spoken a word that she did not choose to take home, and yet which she could not shake off. So she would neither stay in nor go out cheerfully, and sauntered along looking so piteous, that Johnnie could not help making her worse by plucking at her dress, by suddenly twisting her cape round till the back was in front, and pushing her hat over her eyes, till "Don't Johnnie," in a dismal whine, alternated with "I'll tell Miss Fosbrook."

Christabel did not see nor hear. She had gone forward with a boy on either side of her, and Susan walking backwards in front, all telling the story of a cuckoo, - or gowk, as Sara called it in Purday's language, - which they had found in a water-wagtail's nest in a heap of stones; how it sat up, constantly gaping with its huge mouth, while the poor little foster-parents toiled to their utmost to keep it supplied with caterpillars, and the last time it was seen, when full-fledged, were trying to lure it to come out of the nest by holding up green palmers at some little distance before it. This was in the evening; by morning it was gone, having probably taken flight at sunrise.

Miss Fosbrook listened with all the pleasure the boys could desire. She had read natural history, and looked at birds stuffed in the British Museum, or alive at the Zoological Gardens, on the rare days when her father had time to give himself and his children a treat; and her fresh value and interest in all these country things were delightful to the boys.

It was a lovely summer evening. The sun was low enough to make the shadows long and refreshing, as they lay upon the blooming grass of the wilderness, softly swaying in the breeze, all pale with its numerous chaffy blossoms, and varied by the tall buttercups that raised up their shining yellow heads, or by white clouds of bold-faced ox-eye daisies.

The pear-trees were like white garlands; the apple-trees covered with white blossoms and rosy buds; the climbing roses on the wall were bursting into blossom; the sky was one blue vault without a cloud.

Surely Elizabeth had no lack here of what was pretty. Then why did she lag behind, unseeing, unheeding of all, but peevishly pushing off John and Anne, thinking that they always teased her worst on Sundays, and very much discomfited that Miss Fosbrook was not attending to her? Surely the fault was not altogether in what was outside her.

"See!" cry the boys. Miss Fosbrook must first look up there, high upon the side of the house, niched behind that thick stem of the vine. What, can't she see those round black eyes and little beak? They see her plain enough. Ah! now she has them. That's a fly-catcher. By and by they shall be able to show her the old birds flying round, catching flies on the wing, and feeding the young ones, all perched in a row.

Now, can she scramble up the laurels? Yes, she hopes so; though she wished she had known what was coming, for she would have changed her Sunday muslin. But a look of anxiety came on Sam's face as he peeped into the clump of laurels; he signed back the others, sprang upon the dark scraggy bough of the tree, and Hal called out,

"Gone! has Ralph been there?"

"Ay, the black rascal; at least, I suppose so. Not an egg left, and they would have hatched this week!"

"Well, Purday calls him his best friend," said Harry. "He says we should not get a currant or a gooseberry if it wasn't for that there raven, as Papa won't have the small birds shot."

"Bring down the nest, Sam," cried Susan; "Georgy will like to have it."

The children behind, who never could hear of anything to be had without laying a claim to it, shouted that they wanted the nest; but Sam said Sue had spoken first, and they fell back discontented, and more bent on their unkind sport. Miss Fosbrook was rather shocked at the tearing out the nest, and asked if the old bird would not have another brood there; but it was explained that a thrush would never return to a forsaken nest; and when Sam came down with it in his hand, she was delighted with the wonderful cup that formed the lining, so smooth and firm a bason formed of dried mud set within the grassy wall. She had thought that swallows alone built with mud, and had to learn that the swallows used their clay for their outer walls, and down for their lining, whereas the thrush is a regular plasterer.

Sam promised her another thrush to make up for her disappointment, and meantime conducted her to a very untidy old summer-house, the moss of whose roof hung down loose and rough over a wild collection of headless wooden horses, little ships with torn sails, long sticks, battered watering-pots, and old garden tools. She was desired to look up to one of the openings in the ragged moss, and believe that it housed a kitty wren's family of sixteen or eighteen; but she had to take this on trust, for to lay a finger near would lead to desertion; in fact, Sam was rather sorry to be able to point out to her, on coming out, the tiny, dark, nutmeg, cock-tailed father kitty, popping in and out of the thorn hedge, spying at the party.

Now then for a wonder as they came out. Sam waved everybody away - nay, waved is a small word for what he did - shouted, pushed, ordered, would be more like it. He was going to give Miss Fosbrook such a proof of his esteem as hardly any one enjoyed, not even Hal, twice in the summer.

Everybody submitted to his violent demonstrations, and Christabel followed him to the back of the summer-house. There stood a large red flower-pot upside down.

"Now, Miss Fosbrook!"

Sam's finger hooked into the hole at the top. Off came the flower-pot, and disclosed something flying off with rushing wings, and something confused remaining, - a cluster of grey wings all quill, with gaping yellow mouths here and there opening, a huddling movement always going on in the forlorn heap, as if each were cold, and wanted to be undermost.

"Tits , my tits!" said Sam triumphantly; "they've built

Charlotte M. Yonge

their nest here three years following."

"But how do they get in and out?"

"Through the hole. Take care, I'll show you one."

"Won't you frighten away the bird?"

"Oh dear no! Ox-eyes aren't like wrens; I go to them every day. See!" and he took up in his hand a creature that could just be seen to be intended for a bird, though the long skinny neck was bare, and the tiny quills of the young wings only showed a little grey sprouting feather, as did the breast some primrose-coloured down. Miss Fosbrook had to part with some favourite cockney notions of the beauty of infant birds, and on the other hand to gain a vivid idea of what is meant by "callow young."

Sam quickly put his nestling back, and showed her the parent. She could hardly believe that the handsome bird in the smooth grey coat and bright straw-coloured waistcoat, with the broad jet-black line down the centre, the great white cheeks edged with black, and the bold knowing look, could be like what the little bits of deformity in the nest would soon become.

"Ay, that's an ox-eye," said Sam. "You'll hear them going on peter - peter - peter - all the spring."

But Sam was cut short by a loud and lamentable burst of roaring where they had left the party.

Miss Fosbrook hurried back, hearing Hal's rude laugh as she came nearer, it was Elizabeth, sobbing in the passionate way in which it is not good to see a child cry, and violently shaking off Susan, who was begging her to stop herself before Miss Fosbrook should come.

What WAS the matter?

"Oh! Betty's nonsense."

"Johnnie DID -"

"Johnnie only -"

"Now, Hal!"

"Tell-tale!" "Cry-baby!"

"She only cried that Miss Fosbrook might hear."

So shouted the little Babel, Bessie sobbing resentfully between her words, till Miss Fosbrook, insisting that everybody should be quiet, desired her to tell what had happened.

"Johnnie - Johnnie called me a toad."

The others all burst out laughing, and Miss Fosbrook, trying to silence them with a frown, said it was very rude of John, but she saw no reason why a girl of Bessie's age should act so childish a part.

"He's been teasing me, and so has Anne, all this time!" cried Bessie. "They've been at me ever since I came out, pulling me and plaguing me, and -"

"Well," said Susan, "I told you to walk in front of Miss Fosbrook, where they could not."

"I didn't do anything to her," said John.

"Now, Johnnie!"

"He only pulled her frock and poked her ankles," said Anne pleadingly

"Only - and why did you do what she did not like?"

Johnnie looked sturdy and cross. Anne hung her head; and Elizabeth burst out again,

"They always do - they always are cross to me! I said I'd tell you, and now they said Ida was a conceited little toad, and stingy Bet was another;" and out burst her howls again.

"A very sad and improper way of spending a Sunday evening," said Miss Fosbrook, who had really grown quite angry. "Anne and John, I WILL put an end to this teasing. Go to bed this instant."

They did not dare to disobey, but went off slowly with sulky footsteps, muttering to one another that Miss Fosbrook always took pipy Betty's part; Nurse said so, and they wished Mamma was at home. And when they came up to the nursery, Nurse pitied them. She had never heard of a young lady doing such a thing as ordering off two poor dear children to bed for only just saying a word; but it seemed there were to be favourites now. No, she could not put them to bed; they must wait till Mary came in from her walk; she wasn't going to put herself out of the way for any fine London governess.

So Johnnie had another conquest over Miss Fosbrook;

but Anne was uncomfortable, and went and sat in a corner, wishing she had had her punishment properly over, and kicking her brother away when he wanted to play with her.

As for Bessie, she only cried the more for Miss Fosbrook's trying to talk to her. It was a way of hers, perhaps from being less strong than the others, if once she started in a cry she could not leave off.

Susan told Miss Fosbrook so; and the boys tried to drag her on with a promise of a blackbird's nest; but she thought them unfeeling to such woeful distress, and first tried to reason with Bessie, then to soothe her, till at last, finding all in vain, she thought bed the only place for the child, and led her into the house, helped her, still shaking with sobs, to undress, and was going to see her lie down in the bed which she shared with Susan. Elizabeth was still young enough to say her prayers aloud. The words came out in the middle of choking sobs, not as if she were much attending to them. Miss Fosbrook knelt down by her as she was going to rise, and said in her own words,

"Most merciful God, give unto this Thy child the spirit of content, and the spirit of love, that she may bear patiently all the little trials that hurt and vex her, and win her way as Thy good soldier and servant. Amen."

Elizabeth held her breath to listen. It was new and odd. She did not like to say Amen; she did not know if the governess were not taking a liberty. Perhaps it was a new way of telling her she was wrong - Christabel, whom she had thought on her side.

The bad temper woke up, and would not let her offer a

Charlotte M. Yonge

friendly kiss. She hid her face in the pillow, and as soon as Miss Fosbrook had shut the door, went off into a fresh gust of piteous sobs, because Miss Elizabeth Merrifield was the most miserable ill-used child in all the world.

She might be one of the most miserable, but it was not because of her ill-usage, but because she had no spirit to be cheerful, and had turned away from comfort of the right kind. She was in such a frame as to prefer thinking everyone against her, to supposing that anything she could do would mend matters.

Christabel was much grieved at this unfortunate end to the Sunday evening. She looked over all the boys' birds' eggs - they were allowed to keep two of every sort as curiosities - and listened to some wonderful stories of Henry's about climbing trees, and shooting partridges, and she kept the remaining children quiet and amused; but she was not happy in her mind.

She thought she must have been wrong in not watching them more closely, and she felt more dislike and indignation against Johnnie than she feared was altogether right in his governess. Also, she feared to make too much of Elizabeth, and was almost afraid that notice taught her to be still more fretful. And yet there was a sense of being drawn to her by their two minds understanding each other, by likeness of tastes, by pity, and by a wish to protect one whom her little world oppressed.

Nurse Freeman could not be more afraid of Miss Fosbrook making favourites than she was herself.

All she could do in the matter was that which she had

already done at Bessie's bedside, and much more fully than when the little girl was listening to her.

CHAPTER V.

With Monday morning began the earning of the pig. Miss Fosbrook's first business after prayers was to deal out the week's allowance - sixpence to each of the four elders, threepence apiece to the three younger ones.

"May there be no fines," she said.

"I'll not have the hundredth part of a fine!" shouted Henry, tossing his money into the air.

Little David's set lips expressed the same purpose.

"Please let me have a whole sixpence," said Susan. "If I haven't any change, I sha'n't spend it."

"You, Sukey! you'd better have the four farthings," laughed Sam. "You'll be the first to want them."

Susan laughed; and Miss Fosbrook, partly as an example to the plaintive Elizabeth, said, "You are so good-humoured, Susie, that I can't find it in my heart to demand a fine - or - your hair; and there," pointing to the stout red fingers, "did you ever behold such a black little row?"

"Oh dear!" cried Susan, in her good-humoured hearty voice, "how tiresome, when they were SO clean this morning, and I've only just been feeding the chicken, and up in the hay-loft for the eggs, and pulling the radishes!"

"Well, go and wash and brush, and to-morrow remember the pig," said Miss Fosbrook, unable to help comparing the radishes and the fingers for redness and for earthiness.

It was a more difficult matter when, as Elizabeth put her silver coin into her purse, John must needs repeat the stupid old joke, "There goes stingy Bet!" and Bessie put on her woeful appealing face.

"John, I shall punish you if I hear those words again."

"I don't mind. Nurse says you have no business to punish me! She did not put me to bed; and I had such fun! Oh, such fun!" and the boy looked up with a grin that set all the others laughing.

Christabel resolutely kept silence, and hoped her looks did not show her annoyance, as the boy went on, "I got lots of goodies, for Nurse said she had no notion of no stranger punishing her children. Oh! Oh! Oh!" For Samuel had hold of his ear, and was tweaking it sharply.

"There! Go and tell Nurse, if you like, baby!"

"Sam, indeed I can't have my battles fought in that way!" cried the governess, much distressed, as Johnnie roared, perhaps that old Nurse might hear, and, to all attempts to find out whether he were hurt, offered only heels and fists, till Susan came back and hugged him into quiet.

"Now Johnnie has cried before breakfast on a Monday morning," said Annie, "all the rest of the week will go wrong with him."

"Indeed," said Miss Fosbrook, "I hope no such thing. - Suppose we try and show Annie she is wrong, Johnnie!"

But Johnnie was sulky, and even Susan looked as if she thought this a new and dangerous notion. Sam laughed, and said, "I wish you joy, Miss Fosbrook. Now he'll think he must be naughty."

"Johnnie," said David solemnly, "the pig."

The pig was a very good master of the ceremonies, and kept all elbows off the table at breakfast-time; and Bessie, who was apt to stick fast in the midst of her bread and milk, and fall into disgrace for daintiness and dawdling, finished off quietly and prosperously.

Then every one was turned loose till nine o'clock. Susan had charge of Mamma's keys, and had to go down to the kitchen, see what the cook wanted, and put it out, but only on condition that no brother or sister ever went with her to the store-closet. Susan was highly trustworthy, but Mamma was too wise to let her be tempted by voices begging for one plum, one almond, or the last spoonful of Jam. It took away a great deal of the pleasure of jingling the keys, and having a voice in choosing the pudding.

The two elder boys went to their tutor, the other children to the nursery, except Elizabeth, who was rummaging in her little box, and David, whom Miss Fosbrook found perched on the ledge of the window, reading a book that did not look as if it were meant for men of his size.

But Miss Fosbrook thought David like the oldest person in the house - infinitely older than John, who could do nothing better than he except running and bawling, and a good deal older than even Hal and Sam. Nay, there were times when he raised his steady eyes and slowly spoke out his thoughts, when she felt as if he were much more wise and serious than her twenty-years old self.

"Well, Davy," she asked, as at the sound of the lesson-bell the little old man uncrossed his sturdy legs, closed his book, and arose with a sigh, "have you found out all about it?"

"I have found out why a pig is a profitable invest-ment," he answered gravely.

"And why?"

"Because he will feed upon refuse, and fatten upon cheap food," said David, in the words of his book; "only I can't make out why. Do you know, Miss Fosbrook?"

"I don't quite see what you want to know, Davy."

"I want to know why a pig gets fat on barley-meal, when an ox wants mange, and oil-cake and hay. I asked Nurse, and she said little boys mustn't ask questions; and I asked Purday, and he said it was because pigs is pigs, and oxen is oxen. Why do you think it is, Miss Fosbrook?"

"I don't think; I know it is because the great God has made one sort of creature to be easily fed, and made good for poor people to live upon," said Miss Fosbrook.

David's eyes were fixed on her as if he still had questions to ask, and she was quite afraid of her powers of answering them, for he was new in the world, and saw the strangeness of many things to which older people become used by living with them, but which are not the less strange for all that.

However, the trampling of many feet put an end to question and answer, and the day's work had to begin with the Psalms, and reading the Morning Lessons. Bessie was by far the best reader; and David did very well, though he made very long stops to look deliberately at any long new word, and could not bear to be told before he had mastered it for himself. Even Susan was sadly given to gabbling and missing the little words that she thought beneath her attention; and the other two stumbled so horribly, that it was pain to hear them.

This beginning might be taken as the sign of how all would do their lessons. It is only a child here and there, generally a lonely one, to whom lessons can be anything but a toil and an obligation. Even with clever ones, who may be interested in some part of their study, some other branch will be disagreeable; and there is nothing in the whole world to be learnt without drudgery, so it would be unreasonable to expect lessons to be regarded as delightful; but there is one thing that is to be expected of any good child - not to enjoy lessons; not to surpass others; not to do anything surprising; only to make a conscience of doing what is required as well as possible.

Now do not many children seem to think that they are to receive as little as they can possibly take in without being punished; or that, if they make any exertion, their teachers ought to be so much obliged to them, that some great praise or reward is due to them?

Let us see whether anyone in Stokesley school-room was making a conscience of the day's tasks. It is not of much use to ask for any at present in Johnnie - not for a whole week, as Annie would declare; he does not know his single Latin declension; his spelling, is all abroad; his geography wild; yet though turned back once, he misses the fine by just saying his lessons passably the last time. They perhaps ought, in strict justice, to have been sent back; but Miss Fosbrook was very glad to be saved the uproar that would have ensued, and almost wondered whether she were not timidly merciful to the horrible copy and the greasy slate. But Johnnie had no fine, and was as proud of it as if he had been a good boy. "She hadn't caught him out," he said, as if his kind governess had been his enemy.

As to Annie, her French verbs were always dreadful things to hear, and the little merry face, usually so bright, used to grow quite deplorable with the trouble she took not to use her mind. Using her memory was bad enough, but saying things by heart was an affliction she was used to, and it was very shocking of Miss Fosbrook to require her to find out HOW many years Richard II. had reigned, if he began in 1377 and ended in 1399. Susan prompted her, however; so she really got a triumph over Miss Fosbrook, and was quite saved from thinking. Oh, but the teasing woman! she

Charlotte M. Yonge

silenced Susan, and would have this poor injured Annie tell how old the tiresome man was. "Began to reign at eleven years old, dethroned after twenty-two years; how old was he?" Annie found bursting out crying easier than thinking, and then they all cried out, "O Nanny, the pig!" and Miss Fosbrook had the barbarity to call that FOOLISH crying! What might one cry for, if not at being asked how old Richard II. was? If the fine must be paid, there was no use in stopping; so Annie howled till Miss Fosbrook turned her out to finish on the stairs; and as Nurse Freeman was out with the little ones, there was no one to comfort her; so she cried till she was tired, and when the noise ceased, Susan was allowed to come and coax her, and fetch her back to go on with her copy, as soon as her hand was steady enough. She felt very foolish by this time, and thought David eyed her rather angrily and contemptuously; so she crept quietly to her corner, and felt sad and low-spirited all the rest of the morning. Now that thirty-three had come into her head, it seemed so stupid not to have thought of it in time; and then she would have saved her farthing, and her eyes would not have been so hot.

Maybe, too, Susan's French phrases would not have been turned back. Miss Fosbrook would have given a great deal not to have been obliged to do it, but she had prompted flagrantly already, and a teacher is obliged to have a conscience quite as much as a scholar; so the book was given back, and Susan spent twelve minutes in see-sawing herself, and going over the sentences in a rapid whispering gabble, a serious worry to the governess in listening to Bessie's practising and David's reading, but she thought it would be a hardship to be forbidden to learn in her own way at that moment, and forbore. David was interrupted in his

"Little Arthur's History," and looked rather cross about it, for Susan to try again. She made all the same blunders - and more too! Back again! Poor Susie! Once, twice, thrice, has she read those stupid words over, and knows less of them than before. Davy's loud voice will go into her understanding instead of those French phrases. She looks up in dull stupefaction.

William Rufus is disposed of, and David, as grave as a judge, is taking up his slate, looking a little fussed because there is a scratch in the corner. "Well, Susan," says Miss Fosbrook.

Susan jumps up in desperation, and puts her hands behind her. Oh dear! oh dear! all that the gentlemen on a journey were saying to one another has gone clean out of her head!

She cannot recollect the three first words. She only remembers that this is the third time, and another farthing is gone! She stands and stares.

"Susan," says Miss Fosbrook severely, "you never tried to learn this."

Susan gives a little gasp; and Elizabeth, who has said her French without a blunder, puts in an unnecessary and not very sisterly word: "Susan never will learn her French."

Susan's honest eyes fill with tears, but she gulps them back. She will not cry away another farthing, but she does feel it very cross in Bessie, and she is universally miserable.

Christabel feels heated, wearied, and provoked, and as

Charlotte M. Yonge

if she were fast losing her own temper; and that made her resolve on mercy.

"Susie," she said with an effort, "run twice to the great lime-tree and back. Then take the book into my room, read this over three times, and we will try again."

Susan looked surprised, but she obeyed, came back, and repeated the phrases better than she had ever said French before. She was absolutely surprised and highly pleased, and she finished off her other lessons swimmingly; but oh, she was glad to be rid of them! Yes, they were off her mind, and so she deserved that they should be! She flew away to the nursery, and little Sarah was soon crowing in her arms.

Elizabeth? Not a blunder in French verbs or geography - very tidy copy. French reading good; English equally so, only it ended in a pout, because there was not time for her to go on to see what became of Carthage; and she was a most intolerable time in learning her poetry out of the book of Readings, or rather she much preferred reading the verses in other parts of the book to getting perfect in her lesson, and then being obliged to turn her mind to arithmetic. Miss Fosbrook called her three times; and at last she turned round peevishly at being interrupted in the middle of the "Friar of Orders Gray," and repeated her twenty lines of Cowper's "Winter's Walk" in a doleful whine, though without a blunder.

It was one of the horrible novelties that Miss Fosbrook was bringing in, that she expected people to understand their sums as well as work them. She gave much shorter ones, to be sure, than Mamma, who did sometimes set a long multiplication sum of such a huge size, that it looked as if it were meant to keep the victim out of the way; but who would not prefer casting up any length of figures, to being required to explain the meaning of "carrying"?

Really, if it had not been for the pig, that shocking question might have led to a mutiny in the school-room. When it was bad enough to do the thing, how could anyone ask what was meant by the operation, and why it was performed?

What did Bessie do when her sum was being overlooked? Miss Fosbrook read on: "4 from 8, 4; 7 from 1 - how's this, Bessie? 7 from 10 are-"

"3, and 1 are 4," dolorously, as her 3 was changed.

"Now then, what next?"

"Carry one."

"What did I tell you was meant by carry one?"

"The tens," said Bessie, not in the least thinking "the tens" had anything to do with the matter, but only that she had heard something about them, and could thus get rid of the subject.

"Now, Bessie, what tens can you possibly mean? Think a little."

"I'm sure you said tens once," said injured innocence.

"That was in an addition sum. See, here it is quite different. I told you."

Charlotte M. Yonge

Bessie put on a vacant stare. She was not going to attend to what she did not like.

Miss Fosbrook saw the face. She absolutely shrank from provoking another fit of crying, and went quickly through the explanation. She saw that her words might as well have been spoken to the slate. Bessie neither listened nor took them in. Not all her love for her dear Christabel Angela could stir her up to make one effort contrary to her inclinations. The slate was given back to her, she wiped out the sum in a pet, and ran away.

Miss Fosbrook turned round, David, whose lessons had been perfectly repeated an hour ago, was sitting cross-legged in the window, with his slate and pencil, and a basket of bricks, his great delight, which he was placing in rows.

"Miss Fosbrook," said he, "isn't this it? Twelve bricks; take away those seven, then - 1, 2, 3, 4, 5 - the twelve is only 5: the 10 is gone, isn't it? so you must leave one out of the next figure in the upper line of the sum."

Now Davy had only begun arithmetic on the governess's arrival, but he had learnt numeration and addition in her way. She was so delighted, that she stooped down and kissed him, saying, "Quite right, my little man."

Davy rather disapproved of the kiss, and rubbed his brown-holland elbow over his face, as if to clear it off.

"Well," thought Christabel, as she hurried away for five minutes' peace in her own room before the dinner-bell, "it is a comfort to have one pupil whose whole endeavour is not to frustrate one's attempts to educate him."

Poor young thing! that one little bit of sense had quite cheered her up. Otherwise she was not one whit less weary than the children. She had been learning a very tough lesson too - much harder than any of theirs; and she was not at all certain that she had learnt it right.

Now, readers, of all the children, who do you think had used the most conscience at the lessons?

CHAPTER VI.

What an entirely different set of beings were those Stokesley children in lesson-time and out of it! Talk of the change of an old thorn in winter to a May-bush in spring! that was nothing to it!

Poor, listless, stolid, deplorable logs, with bowed backs and crossed ankles, pipy voices and heavy eyes! Who would believe that these were the merry, capering, noisy creatures, full of fun and riot, clattering and screeching, and dancing about with ecstasy at Sam's information that there was a bonfire by the potato-house!

"A bonfire!" said the London governess, thinking of illuminations; "what can that be for?"

"Oh, it is not FOR anything," said Susan; "it is Purday burning weeds. Don't you smell them? How nice they are! I was afraid it was only Farmer Smith burning couch."

All the noses were elevated to scent from afar a certain smoky odour, usually to be detected in July breezes, and which reminded Miss Fosbrook of a brick-field.

"Potatoes! Potatoes! We'll roast some potatoes, and have them for tea!" bellowed all the voices; so that

Miss Fosbrook could hardly find a space for very unwillingly saying,

"But, my dears, I don't know whether I ought to let you play with fire."

"Oh, we always do," roared the children; and Susan added,

"We always roast potatoes when there's a bonfire. Mamma always lets us; it is only Purday that is cross."

"Yes, yes; Mamma lets us."

"Well, if Sam and Susan say it is right, I trust to them," said Miss Fosbrook gladly; "only you must let me come out and see what it is. I am too much of a Londoner to know."

"Oh yes; and we'll roast you some potatoes."

So the uproarious population tumbled upstairs, there to be invested with rougher brown-holland garments than those that already concealed the sprigged cottons of the girls; and when the five came down again, they were so much alike in dress, that it was not easy to tell girls from boys. Susan brought little George down with her, and off the party set. Sam and Hal, who had been waiting in the hall, took Miss Fosbrook between them, as if they thought it their duty to do the honours of the bonfire, and conducted her across the garden, through the kitchen-garden, across which lay a long sluggish bar of heavy and very odorous smoke, to a gate in a quickset hedge. Here were some sheds and cart-houses, a fagot pile, various logs of timber, a grindstone, and - that towards which all the eight children rushed with

Charlotte M. Yonge

whoops of ecstasy - a heap of smoking rubbish, chiefly dry leaves, and peas and potato haulm, with a large allowance of cabbage stumps - all extremely earthy, and looking as if the smouldering smoke were a wonder from so mere a heap of dirt.

No matter! There were all the children round it, some on their knees, some jumping; and voices were crying on all sides,

"O jolly, jolly!" "I'll get some potatoes!" "Oh, you must have some sticks first, and make some ashes." "There's no flame - not a bit!" "Get out of the way, can't you? I'll make a hot place." "We'll each have our own oven, and roast our own potatoes!" "Don't, Sam; you're pushing me into the smoke!"

This of course was from Elizabeth; and there followed, "Don't, Bessie, you will tread upon Georgie. - Yes, Georgie, you SHALL have a place."

"Sticks, sticks!" shouted Henry; while Sam was on his knees, poking out a species of cavern in the fire, where some symptoms of red embers appeared, which he diligently puffed with his mouth, feeding it with leaves and smaller chips in a very well practised way. "Sticks, Annie! Johnnie! Davy! get sticks, I say, and we'll make an oven."

Annie obeyed; but the two little boys were intent on imitating Sam on another side of the fire, and Johnnie uttered a gruff "Get 'em yourself," while David took no notice at all.

Perhaps Hal would have betaken himself to no gentle means if Susan had not hastily put in his way a plentiful supply of dead wood, which she had been letting little George think he picked up all himself; and there was keen excitement, which Christabel could not help sharing, while under Sam's breath the red edges of the half-burnt chip glowed, flushed, widened, then went sparkling doubtfully, slowly, to the light bit of potato-stalk that he held to it, glowing as he blew - fading, smoking, when he took breath. Try again - puff, puff, puff diligently; the fire evidently has a taste for the delicate little shaving that Annie has found for it; it seizes on it; another - another; a flame at last. Hurrah! pile on more; not too much. "Don't put it out!" Oh, there! strong flame - coming crackling up through those smothering heaps of stick and haulm; it won't be kept down; it rises in the wind; it is a red flaring banner. The children shriek in transports of admiration, little George loudest of all, because Susan is holding him tight, lest he should run into the brilliant flame. Miss Fosbrook is rather appalled, but the children are all safe on the windward side, and seem used to it; so she supposes it is all right, and the flame dies down faster than it rose. It is again an innocent smouldering heap, like a volcano after an eruption.

"We must not let it blaze again just yet," said Sam; "keep it down well with sticks, to make some nice white ashes for the potatoes. See, I'll make an oven."

They were all stooping round this precious hot corner, some kneeling, some sitting on the ground, David with hands on his sturdy knees - all intent on nursing that creeping red spark, as it smouldered from chip to chip, leaving a black trace wherever it went, when through the thick smoke, that was like an absolute curtain hiding everything on the farther side, came headlong a huge bundle of weeds launched overwhelmingly on the

Charlotte M. Yonge

fire, and falling on the children's heads in an absolute shower, knocking Johnnie down, but on a soft and innocent side of the fire among the cabbage-stumps, and seeming likely to bury Sam, who leant over to shelter his precious oven, and puffed away as if nothing was happening, amid the various shouts around him, in which "Purday" was the most audible word.

"Ah, so you've got at he, after all," said Purday, leaning on the fork with which he had thrown on the weeds. "Nothing is safe from you."

"What, you thought you had a new place, Purday, and circumvented us!" cried Hal; "but we smelt you out, you old rogue; we weren't going to be baulked of our bonfire."

Miss Fosbrook here ventured on asking if they were doing mischief; and Purday answered with an odd gruff noise, "Mischief enough - ay, to be sure - hucking the fire all abroad. It's what they're always after. I did think I'd got it safe out of their way this time."

"Then," in rather a frightened voice, for she felt that it would be a tremendous trial of her powers, "should I make them come away?"

"Catch her!" muttered Hal.

There was horror and disapprobation on Susan's face. Annie stood with her mouth open; while John, throwing himself on the ground with fury, rolled over, crying out something about, "I won't," and "very cross;" and David lay flat on his face, puffing at his own particular oven, like a little Wind in an old picture. Sam waited, leaning on the ashen stick that served him as a poker. It was the most audacious thing he had ever heard. Rob them of their bonfire! Would that old traitor of a Purday abet her?

Perhaps Purday was as much astonished as the rest; but, after all, much as the children tormented his bonfires, overset his haycocks, and disturbed his wood-pile, he did not like anyone to scold them but himself, much less the new London Lady; so he made up an odd sort of grin, and said, "No, no, Ma'am, it ain't that they do so much harm; let 'em bide;" and he proceeded to shake on the rest of his barrowful, tumbling the weeds down over David's cherished oven in utter disregard; but the children cried with one voice, "Hurrah! hurrah! Purday, we don't do any harm, so don't ever grumble again. Hurrah!"

"And I don't care for HER, the crosspatch," said Johnnie to Annie, never hearing or heeding Miss Fosbrook's fervent "I am so glad!"

And as long as the foolish boy remembered it, he always did believe that Miss Fosbrook was so cross as to want to hinder them from their bonfire, only Purday would not let her.

Miss Fosbrook did not trouble herself to be understood; she was relieved to have done her duty, and be free to rejoice in and share the pleasure. She ran about and collected materials for Sam till she was out of breath, and joined in all the excitement as the fire showed symptoms of reviving, after being apparently crushed out by Purday. Sam and Susan, at least, believed that she had only spoken to Purday because she thought it right; but even for them to forgive interference with their bonfire privileges was a great stretch.

At last she thought it time to leave them to their own devices, and seize the moment for some quiet reading; but she had not reached the house before little steps came after her, and she saw Elizabeth running fast.

"They are so tiresome," she said. "Sam won't let me stand anywhere but where the smoke gets into my eyes, and George plagues so! May I come in with you, dear Christabel?"

"You are very welcome," said Miss Fosbrook, "but I am sorry to hear so many complaints."

"They are so cross to me," said Bessie; "they always are."

"You must try to be cheerful and good-humoured with them, and they will leave off vexing you."

"But may I come in? It will be a nice time for my secret."

Christabel saw little hope for her intended reading, but she was always glad of a space for making Bessie happy, so she kindly consented to the bringing out of the little girl's treasury, and the dismal face grew happy and eager. The subjects of the drawings were all clear in her head; that was not the difficulty, but the cardboard, the ribbon, the real good paints. One little slip of card Miss Fosbrook hunted out of her portfolio; she cut a pencil of her own, and advised the first attempt to be made upon a piece of paper. The little bird that Bessie produced was really not at all bad, and her performance was quite fair enough to make it worth while to go on, since Miss Fosbrook well knew that mammas are pleased with works of their children, showing more good-will than skill. For why? Their value is in the love and thought they show.

The little bird was made into a robin with the colours in a paint-box that Bessie had long ago bought; but they were so weak and muddy, that the result was far from good enough for a present, and it was agreed that real paints must be procured as well as ribbon. Miss Fosbrook offered to commission her sisters to buy the Prussian blue, lake, and gamboge in London, and send them in a letter. This was a new idea to Bessie, and she was only not quite decided between the certainty that London paints must be better than country ones, and the desire of the walk to Bonchamp to buy some; but the thought that the ribbon, after all, might be procured there, satisfied her. The little doleful maid was changed into an eager, happy, chattering child, full of intelligence and contrivance, and showing many pretty fancies, since there was no one to tease her and laugh at her; and her governess listened kindly and helpfully.

Miss Fosbrook could not help thinking how much happier her little companion would have been as an only child, or with one sister, and parents who would have made the most of her love of taste and refinement, instead of the hearty busy parents, and the rude brothers and sisters, who held her cheap for being unlike themselves. But then she bethought her, that perhaps Bessie might have grown up vain and affected, had all these tastes been petted and fostered, and that perhaps her little hardships might make her the stronger, steadier, more useful woman, instead of living in fancies. It was the unkindness on one side, and the temper on the other, that made Miss Fosbrook uneasy.

The work had gone on happily for nearly an hour, and Bessie was copying a forget-me-not off a little painted card-board pincushion of her own, when steps were heard, little trotting steps, and Susan came in with little George. He had been pushed down by Johnnie, and was rather in a fretful mood; and Susan had left all her happy play to bring him in to rest and comfort him, coming to the school-room because Nurse Freeman was out. Before Elizabeth had time to hide away her doings, George had seen the bright pincushion, and was holding out his hands for it. Bessie hastily pocketed it. George burst out crying; and Susan, without more ado, threw herself on her sister, and, pinioning Bessie's slight arm by the greater strength of her firm one, was diving into her pocket in spite of her struggles.

"Susan, leave off," said Miss Fosbrook; "let your sister alone. She has a right to do what she likes with her own."

"It is so cross in her," said Susan, obeying however, but only to snatch up little George, and hug and kiss him. "Poor dear little man! is Betty cross to him? There! there! come with Sue, and SHE'LL get him something pretty."

"Susie, Susie, indeed it's only that I don't want him to spoil it," said Elizabeth, distressed.

"A foolish thing like that! Why, the only use of it is to please the children; but you are just such a baby as he is," said Susan, still pitying George.

"You had better put your things away, Bessie," said Miss Fosbrook, interfering to stop the dispute; and as soon as Elizabeth was gone, and George a little pacified by an ivory ribbon-measure out of Miss Fosbrook's work-box, she observed to Susan, "My dear, you must not let your love for the little ones make you unjust and unkind to Bessie."

"She always is so unkind to them," said Susan resentfully.

"I don't think she feels unkindly; but if you tyrannize over her, and force her to give way to them, you cannot expect her to like it."

"Mamma says the elder must give way to the younger," said Susan.

"You did not try whether she would give way."

"No, because I knew she wouldn't; and I could not have my little Georgie vexed."

"And I could not see my little Susie violent and unjust," said Miss Fosbrook cheerfully. "Justice first, Susan; you had no right to rob Bessie for George, any more than I should have to give away a dinner of your papa's because he had refused a beggar."

"Papa never would," said Susan, rather going off from the point.

"Very likely; but do you understand me, Susan? I will not have Bessie FORCED out of her rights for the little ones. Not Bessie only, but nobody is to be tyrannized over; it is not right."

"Bessie is so nonsensical," was all Susan said, looking glum.

"Very likely she may seem so to you; but if you knew more, you would see that all is not nonsense that seems so to you. Some people would admire her ways."

"Yes, I know," said Susan. "Mrs. Greville told Mrs. Brownlow that Bessie was the only one among us that was capable of civilisation; but Mrs. Greville is a fine lady, and we always laugh at her."

"And now," as Bessie returned, "you want to go out to your play again, my dear. Will you leave Georgie with us?"

Susan was a little doubtful about trusting her darling with anyone, especially one who could take Bessie's part against him; but she wished exceedingly to be present at the interesting moment of seeing whether the potatoes were done enough, and George was perfectly contented with measuring everything on the ribbon, so she ran quickly off, without the manners to thank Miss Fosbrook, but to assure the rest of the party that the governess really was very good-natured, and that she would save her biggest and best potato for Miss Fosbrook's tea.

Christabel managed very happily with little George, though not quite without offending Elizabeth, who thought it very hard to be desired to put away her painting instead of tantalizing her little brother with the sight of what he must not have. Miss Fosbrook could not draw her into the merry game with little George, which made his shouts of glee ring out through the house, and meet Nurse Freeman's ear as she came indoors with the baby, and calling at the school-room door, summoned him off to his tea, as if she were in a pet with Miss Fosbrook for daring to meddle with one of HER own nursery children.

Nothing more was heard of the others, and Christabel and Elizabeth both read in peace till the tea-bell rang, and they went down and waited and waited, till Miss Fosbrook accepted Bessie's offer of going out to call the rest. But Bessie returned no more than the rest; and the governess set forth herself, but had not made many steps before the voices of the rabble rout were heard, and they all were dancing and clattering about her, while Susan and Hal each carried aloft a plate containing articles once brown, now black, and thickly powdered with white ashes, as were the children themselves up to their very hair.

As a slight concession to grown-up people's prejudices, they did, at the risk of their dear potatoes getting cold, scamper up to perform a species of toilette, and then sat down round the tea-table, Susie, David, and Sam each vociferous that Miss Fosbrook should eat "my potato that I did on purpose for her." Poor Miss Fosbrook! she would nearly as soon have eaten the bonfire itself as those cinder-coated things, tough as leather outside, and within like solid smoke. Indeed the children, who had been bathing in smoke all day, had brought in the air of it with them; but their tongues ran fast on their adventures, and their taste had no doubt that their own bonfire potatoes were the most perfect cookery in art! Miss Fosbrook picked out the most eatable bits of each of the three, and managed to satisfy the three cooks, all zealous for their own. Other people's potatoes might be smoky, but each one's own was delicious - "quite worthy of the pig when he was bought," thought Miss Fosbrook; but she made her real pleasure at the kind feeling to cover her dislike of the black potatoes, and thus pleased the children without being untrue.

"Line upon line, precept upon precept; here a little, and there a little." That is the way habits are formed and characters made; not all at once. So there had been an opportunity for Susan to grow confirmed in her kindness and unselfishness, as well as to learn that tyranny is wrong, even on behalf of the weak; and Bessie, if she would take home the lesson, had received one in readiness to be cheerful, and to turn from her own pursuits to oblige others. Something had been attempted toward breaking her habit of being fretful, and thinking herself injured. It remained to be seen whether the many little things that were yet to happen to the two girls would be so used as to strengthen their good habits or their bad ones.

CHAPTER VII.

It is not worth while to go on describing every day at Stokesley, since lessons were far too much alike; and play-times, though varied enough for the house of Merrifield, might be less entertaining to the readers.

Enough to say, that by Saturday afternoon John had not only forfeited his last farthing, but was charged with another into next week, for the poor pleasure of leaving his hat on the school-room floor because Elizabeth had told him of it. At about four o'clock it set in for rain, catching the party at some distance from home, so that, though they made good speed, the dust turned into mud, and clung fast to their shoes.

David, never the best runner, was only in time to catch Johnnie by the skirt upon the third step of the staircase, crying out, "The pig!" but Johnnie, tired of the subject, and in a provoking mood, twitched away his pinafore, crying, "Bother the pig!" and rushed up after the four who had preceded him, leaving such lumps of dirt on the edge of every step, that when Miss Fosbrook came after with Elizabeth she could not but declare that a shower was a costly article.

"You see," observed Susan, "when it's such fine weather it puts one's feet out of one's head."

Charlotte M. Yonge

While Sam, Henry, and Bessie were laughing at Susan for this speech, little George trotted in, crying out, "Halty man come, Halty man come; Georgie want sweetie!"

"The Gibraltar man!" cried John and Annie with one voice, and they were at the bottom of the stairs with a bound.

"Oh, send him away, send him away. They'll spend all their money, and there will be none left!" was David's cry; while George kept dragging his eldest sister's frock, with entreaties of "Susie, Susie, come."

"They call him the Gibraltar man, because he sells Gibraltar rock, and gingerbread, and all those things," said Henry in explanation. "We have always dealt with him; and he is very deserving; and his wife makes it all - at least I know she makes ginger-beer - so we must encourage him."

So Henry hastened downstairs to encourage the Gibraltar man; and Susan, saying soothingly, "Yes, yes, Georgie; - never mind Davie, we'll make up for it; I can't vex him," had taken the little fellow in her arms and followed.

"Pigs enough here, without sending to the fair," muttered Sam.

"Please, Sam, please, Miss Fosbrook, send the Gibraltar man away, and don't let him come," cried David quite passionately. "Nasty man! He will come every Saturday, and they'll always spend all their money."

"But, my friend," said Miss Fosbrook good-humouredly, "suppose we have no right to banish the Gibraltar man?"

"*I* don't wan't him," said Bessie; "it makes my fingers sticky."

"You're no good," said David vehemently. "I don't like you, and I hate the Gibraltar man, taking away all our money from poor Hannah."

"Gently, gently, Davie; nobody makes you spend your money; and perhaps the poor man has children of his own who want food as much as Hannah's do."

"Then can't they eat the Gibraltar rock and bulls' eyes?"

Sam suggested that this diet would make them sick; to which poor little earnest David answered, that when once the pig was bought, he would give all his money for a whole month to the Gibraltar man, if he would not come for the next four weeks.

And Christabel thought of what she had once read, that people would often gladly put away from their children friends the very trials that are sent by Heaven to prove and strengthen their will and power of resisting self-indulgence. Before she had quite thought it out, the quick steps were back again, and Sam greeted the entrance of John thus: "Well, if that isn't a shame! Have you been and done Sukey out of all that, Jack?"

"It was only three bulls' eyes," said Susan, following. "You know he had nothing of his own, and it was so hard, and Annie gave him some."

Charlotte M. Yonge

"And Nurse some," added Hal. "Trust Jackie for taking care of himself." Well he might say so, considering how full were John's mouth, hands, and pockets.

"And Davie has had nothing!" said kind Susan. "Here, Davie!" holding out to him an amber-like piece of barley-sugar.

"I don't want your stuff," said David roughly. "You've spent all away from the pig."

"No, Davie, indeed, only twopence," said Susan; "pray have a bit."

"You might at least say thank you," said Miss Fosbrook.

But how difficult is that middle road which is the only right one! David, being too much set on one single purpose, good though it was, could see nothing else. It was right and generous to abstain from sweets with this end in view; but it was wrong to be rude and unthankful to the sister who meant all so kindly, and was the most unselfish of all. She turned round to Elizabeth with the kind offer of the dainty she had not even tasted herself, but was not more graciously treated.

"How can you, Susie? it is all pulled about with your fingers."

This was a matter on which the Misses and Masters Merrifield were not wont to be particular; and with one of the teasing laughs that Bessie hated, Sam exclaimed as Susan turned to him, "Yes, thank you, Sukey, *I* don't mind finger sauce," but not before John was stretching out a hand glazed with sugar, and calling out, "Oh, give it to me!" and as it disappeared in his brother's mouth, he burst out angrily, "How cross, Sam! You did that on purpose!"

"Yes," said Sam, "I did; for though pigs on four legs are all very well, I don't like pigs on two."

"Here, Jackie, never mind," said Susan, seeing him about to begin to cry, and offering him her last sugar-plum.

"I don't want sugar-plums, I want barley-sugar," said John devouring it nevertheless.

"I haven't one bit more," said Susan regretfully.

"Have you had any yourself, Susan?" asked Sam.

"No; but I didn't want any."

"Oh then, here Susie, I always keep a reserve," said Henry. "No, no, not you, Jack; I don't feed little pigs, whatever Susie does."

And in spite of Susan, both the elder brothers set on John, teasing him about his greediness, till he burst out crying, and ran away to the nursery. Miss Fosbrook hated the teasing, but she thought it served John so rightly, that she would not save him from it; and she only interfered to remind the others that their fingers would bring them in for fines unless they were washed before tea.

"And how much have you spent?" reproachfully asked that rigid young judge, David; but all the answer he got was a pull by the hair from Hal, and "Hollo, young

Charlotte M. Yonge

one! am I to give my accounts to you?"

David gravely put up his hand and smoothed his ruffled locks, repeating, in his manful way, "I want to know what you have left for the pig?"

Whereupon Hal laid hold of him, pulled him off the locker, and rolled him about on the floor like a puppy dog, crying, "I'll tell you what, if you make such a work about it, I'll spend all my allowance, and not subscribe at all."

"Sam!" cried the tormented David, and "Sam!" cried the governess, really afraid the little boy would be hurt; but Sam only stood laughing with his back to the shutter, and Christabel herself hurried to the rescue, to pick Henry off his victim, holding an arm tight, while the child got up, and ran away to get his hair re-brushed for tea.

"Now, Hal, you might have hurt him," argued the governess.

"Very good thing for him too," said the brothers with one voice.

She was very much shocked; but when she thought it over she perceived that though Hal might be to blame, yet in the long run even this rough discipline might be more useful to her dear little David than being allowed to take upon him with his elder brothers, and grow conceited and interfering.

Miss Fosbrook was not surprised when, next morning, a frightful bellowing was heard instead of Johnnie being seen, and she learnt that Master John was in the hands of Nurse Freeman, who was administering to him a dose in consequence of his having been greatly indisposed all night. It must be confessed that Christabel was not very sorry to hear it, nor that Nurse would keep him to herself all day; for bad company as Johnnie had been on the week-days, he had been worse on the Sunday.

And when John came out on Monday, he looked like a different boy; he had lost his fractious, rebellious look; he spoke as civilly as could be expected of a small Merrifield, and showed no signs of being set against his lessons. To be sure it was a bad way of spending a Sunday, to be laid up with ailments brought on by over-eating; but even this was better than spending it, like the former one, in wilful misbehaviour; and John, who knew that Papa, Mamma, brothers, and sisters all alike detested and despised real greediness, had been heartily ashamed of himself, both for this and his forfeits. A new week was a new starting-point, and he meant to spend this one well. For indeed it is one of the blessings of our lives that we have so many stages - days, weeks, years, and the like - from each of which we may make fresh starts, feel old things left behind, and go on to lead a new life.

Besides, Johnnie was quite well now; and perhaps no child, so well brought up, could have been so constantly naughty the whole week without some degree of ailment, suspected neither by himself nor others. For this is one of our real troubles, when either young or old, that sometimes there is a feeling of discomfort and vexation about us that, without knowing why, makes everything go amiss, causes everybody else to appear cross, and all tasks, all orders, all misadventures, to become great grievances. Grown-up people feel this as well as children; but they have gone through it often enough to know what is the matter, and they have, or ought to have, more self-command. But children have yet to learn by experience that the outer things are not harder and more untoward, so much as that they themselves are out of sorts. This is poor comfort; and certainly it is dangerous to say to ourselves that being poorly is any excuse for letting ourselves be cross, or for not doing our best. If Mrs. Merrifield had thought so, what miserable lives her husband and children would have led! No, the way to use the certain fact that the state of our bodies affects our tempers and spirits, is to say to ourselves, "Well, if this person or this thing do seem disagreeable, or if this work, or even this little bit of obedience, be very tiresome, perhaps it may really be only a fancy of mine, and if I go to it with a good will, I may work off the notion;" or, "Perhaps I am cross to-day, let me take good care how I answer." And a little prayer in our hearts will be the best help of all. Self-command and goodness will not come by nature as we grow up, but we must work for them in childhood.

When the Monday allowances were brought out, and the pig's chance inquired into, David alone produced his whole sum, untouched by forfeiture or waste, and dropped it into "Toby Fillpot." Elizabeth had her entire sixpence; but a penny had been spent on a letter to Mamma, and she gave but one to the fund, in spite of the black looks she met from David. Sam had lost a farthing by the shower, and had likewise bought a queen's head, to write to his father. The rest, four-pence-three farthings, he paid over. Poor Johnnie! his last week's naughtiness had exceeded his power of paying fines, and a halfpenny was subtracted from this week's threepence; while the Gibraltar man had consumed all that fines had spared to little Annie, had left Susan only threepence, and Henry but twopence-halfpenny. This, with twopence that Miss Fosbrook had found in her travelling-bag, made one shilling and fourpence-farthing - a very poor collection for one week. David was quite melancholy.

"Never mind," said Henry; "Mr. Carey's brother, the Colonel, is coming to stay here the last week in July, and he gives us boys half-a-sovereign each, so that we might buy a stunning pig all ourselves twice over."

"Always? He never did so but once," said Sam.

"That was the only time he saw us, though," said Hal; "and we were quite little boys then. I'll tell you what, Sam, he'll give us each a sovereign this time, and then I'll buy a bow and arrows."

"Stuff!" said Sam. "I hope he won't."

"Why not?"

"I hate it! I hate saying thank you; I shall get out of the way, if I can."

"Sam has no manners!" said Hal, turning round to Miss Fosbrook. "To think that he had rather go without a sovereign or two than say thank you!"

"I'M too much of a gentleman to lay myself out for presents!" retorted Samuel; and the two boys fell on each other, buffeting one another, all in good part on Sam's side, though there was some temper and annoyance on Henry's.

When Sam was out of hearing, Hal discoursed very grandly on the sovereign he intended Colonel Carey to give him, and the prodigious things he meant to do with it. A gentleman once gave Osmond Greville two sovereigns; why should not Colonel Carey be equally liberal? And to hear the boy, those two sovereigns would buy everything in the world, from the pig to a double-barrelled gun. David began to grow hurt, and to fear the Toby fund would be lost in this magnificence; but Hal assured him that it would be a help, and they should all have a share in the pig, promising presents to everybody, which Susan and Annie expected with the more certainty that Sam was never present to laugh down these fine projects.

Indeed Miss Fosbrook had laughed at them once or twice, and observed that she thought money earned or spared a better thing than money given; and this caused Hal to cease to try to dazzle her, though he could not give up the pleasure of regaling his sisters in private with the wonders to be done with Colonel Carey's possible sovereigns.

CHAPTER VIII.

The second week was prosperous: the treasury made progress; and Christabel began to feel as if her pupils were not beyond her management, as at first she had feared. Collectively they were less uncouth and bearish, not so noisy at their meals, nor so needlessly rude to one another; and the habit of teasing Elizabeth whenever there was nothing else to do was greatly lessened. Indeed Sam did not plague her himself, nor let his brothers do so, unless she tempted him by some very foolish whine or bit of finery; and in such eases a little friendly merriment is a sound cure, very unlike the hateful fault of tormenting for tormenting's sake.

Nor did Elizabeth give nearly so much cause for their rough laughter, since Miss Fosbrook had given wholesome food to her tastes and likings, partly satisfying the longing for variety, beauty, or interest which had made her discontented and restless. Her head was full of HER secret, and her pretty plans for her gift. Such lovely drawings she saw in her mind's eye, such fairies, such delightful ships, kittens, babies in the cradle! But when the pencil was in her hand, the lines went all ways but the right; her fairy was a grimy little object, whose second wing could never be put on; the ships were saucers; the kitten might have been the pig; the baby was an owl in an ivy-bush; and to look at the live baby in the cradle only puzzled her the more. Miss

Charlotte M. Yonge

Fosbrook gave her real drawing lessons; but boxes, palings, and tumble-down sheds, done with a broad black pencil, did not seem to help her to what she wished. Yet sometimes her fingers produced what surprised and pleased herself and Christabel; and she never was happier than when safely shut into Miss Fosbrook's bed-room with her card and her paints. She used to bolt herself in, with a little parade of mystery that made Annie exceedingly curious, though the others generally let it alone as "Betty's fancy."

Christabel wanted to learn botany for her own pleasure. She found a book which Susan and Bessie pronounced to be horridly stupid (indeed Annie called it nasty, and was reproved for using such a word), but when the information in it was minced up small, and brought out in a new form, Bessie enjoyed it extremely. The whole party were delighted to gather flowers for Miss Fosbrook - the wetter or the steeper places they grew in the better; but the boys thought it girlish to know the names; and Susan, though liking gardening, did not in the least care for the inside of a flower. Elizabeth, however, was charmed at the love-liness that was pointed out to her; and even Annie, when the boys were not at hand, thought it very entertaining to look at petals, stamens, and pistils, and to see that a daisy is made up of a host of tiny flowers. Both little sisters were having their eyes opened to see some of the wonder and some of the glory of this earth of ours. It made Bessie much less often tired of everything and everybody; though after all there is but one spirit that is certain never to be weary or dissatisfied, and into that she had yet to grow.

Fines were much less frequent: there were no foolish tears; only one lesson of John's turned back, two of

Annie's, one of Susan's; some unbrushed hair of Susan's too - an unlucky mention of the raven by Annie in lesson-time - and some books left about by Sam. Henry's fines were the serious ones: he had two for incorrect sums, one for elbows on the table, three for talking, one for not putting his things away; and besides, he COULD NOT go without a pennyworth of string; and the Grevilles would have laughed at him if he had not bought some more marbles.

But what did that signify when Colonel Carey was coming? and a sovereign would buy a pig three times over - at least, if it was quite a little one. Christabel wished the hope of that sovereign had never occurred to him, for he seemed to think it quite set him free from the little self-restraints by which the others were earning the pleasure of making the gift; and though he still talked the most about the pig, he denied himself the least for it.

One evening the boys came in with a great piece of news. Their tutor had read in the paper that Admiral Penrose was appointed to the Ramilies, to take command in the Mediterranean. He was a great friend of their father, and, said the boys, was most likely to make him his flag-captain.

"And me a naval cadet!" said Hal. "He said he would, when he was here!"

"One of you, he said," put in Susan.

"I know it will be me!" said Hal. "He looked at the rigging of my frigate, and said I knew all the ropes quite well; and he told Papa he might be proud of such a son!"

"Oh! oh!" groaned the aggrieved multitude.

"Well - such a family; but he was looking at me; and I know he will give me the appointment; and I shall sail in his ship - you'll see. And when I get to the Mediterranean, I'll tell you what I'll do - I shall kill a shark all my own self!"

"A shark in the Mediterranean!"

"Well, why shouldn't they get in by the Straits of Magellan? Oh! Is that the other place? Well, never mind - I'll shoot the shark."

"Stuff, Hal!" said Sam rather gruffly.

Hal went off on another tack. "Well, at least he has set me down by this time; and Papa will have me up to London for my outfit."

"I hope you will have leave, and come and see us," said Annie.

"I'll try; but, you see, I shall be an officer on duty, and I dare say Admiral Penrose will hardly be able to spare me; but I'll send you all presents out of my pay."

"You'll spend all your pay on yourself," said David.

"Out of my prize-money then."

"You can't get prize-money without a war," said Elizabeth.

"Oh! don't let there be a war!" cried Susan.

"Yes, but there is!" said Harry in a tremendous tone; and as Miss Fosbrook held up her hands, "at least there was one in the Black Sea; and I know there was a battle in the newspaper - at least, Mr. Carey read about Palermo."

"I don't think Garibaldi in Sicily will put much prize-money into your pocket, Hal," said Miss Fosbrook.

"Oh! but there's sure to be a war! and I shall get promoted, and be a man before any of you. I shall go about, and see condors, and lions, and elephants, and wear a sword - at least, a dirk - while you are learning Latin and Greek at Uncle John's!"

"Don't make such a noise about it!" said Sam crossly.

"I don't know why you should be the one to go," said Elizabeth. "Sam is the eldest."

"Yes; but Sam is such a slow-coach. Papa said I was the only one fit to make a sailor of - at least, he said I was smart, and - Hollo! Sam, I won't have you kicking my legs!"

"Don't keep up such a row then!" growled Sam; but Hal was in too full swing to be reached by slight measures. He pushed his chair back, tucked up his feet like a tailor's, out of reach, and went on: "Then I shall come home in my cocked hat, like Papa's - at least, my cap - and come and ask for a holiday for you all at Uncle John's."

Uncle John was an under-master at one of the great public schools, and the children were all a good deal in awe of him.

Charlotte M. Yonge

"Uncle John won't give one for YOU!" said Sam.

"Come, boys, I can't have this bickering," said Miss Fosbrook. "I can't see you trying which can be most provoking. Stand up. Now, David, say grace. There, Annie, finish that bit of bread out of doors. Go out, and let us have no more of this."

She spoke now with much less fear of not being minded; and having seen one of the quarrelsome parties safe out of the school-room, she went to fetch from her own room a glove that wanted mending; and on her return found Sam alone there, curled up over his lesson-books on the locker, looking so gloomy, that she was afraid she had made him sulky, for which she would have been very sorry, since she had a respect for him.

"What is the matter?" she asked; and his "Nothing" did not at all assure her that he was in a right mood. She doubted whether to leave him alone; but presently thought he looked more unhappy than ill-tempered, and ventured to speak. "Have you a hard piece to learn? Perhaps I could help you."

He let her come and look at his book; but, to her surprise, he had before him a very easy problem in Euclid.

"Indeed, if you only gave your mind to this," she said, "you would soon make it out."

"Stupid stuff!" exclaimed Sam. "It is all along of that, and the rest of it, that I have got to be a land-lubber!" and he threw the book to the other end of the room.

"Have you no chance?" said Miss Fosbrook, without taking notice of this rudeness, for she saw that the boy could hardly contain himself.

"No! The Admiral did take notice of Hal; and one day when I was slow at a proposition, my father said I was too block-headed to beat navigation into, and that Hal is a smart fellow, worth two of me. I know he is! I know that; only if he would not make such an intolerable crowing - "

"Then you wish it very much?"

"Wish it! Of course I do. Why, my father is a sailor; and I remember the Fury, and I saw the Calliope - his ship that he had in the war time. Before I was as big as little George I always thought I should be a sailor. And now if Papa goes out with Admiral Penrose, and Hal too - oh! it will be so horrid home!"

"But can't you both go?"

"No; my father said he couldn't ask to have two of us put down, unless perhaps some younger one had a chance by and by. And Hal is the sharpest, and does everything better than I can when he has a mind. My father says, among so many all can't choose; and if this place is to be mine, Hal may want to be in the navy more than I. Yes, it is all right, and Hal must go. But - but - when my father is gone - "and Sam fairly burst out crying. "I didn't hardly know how different it is with him away till this month. I was such a little fellow when he went to the Black Sea; but now - never mind, though!" and he stamped his foot on the floor. "Papa said it, and it must be. Don't tell the others, Miss Fosbrook;" and he resolutely went and picked up his

Euclid, and began finding the place.

"You will do your duty like a man, wherever you are, Sam," said Christabel heartily.

Sam looked as if he had rather that she had not said it, but it was comfortable to him for all that; and though she kept further compliments to herself, she could not but think that there was no fear but that he would be a man, in the best sense of the word, before Hal, when she saw him so manfully put his sore grievance out of his head, and turn to the present business of conquering his lesson. Nor did she hear another word from him about his disappointment.

It made her dislike Henry's boasts more than ever; and she used to cut them short as fast as she could, till the young chatterer decided that she was "cross," and reserved all his wonderful "at leasts" for his sisters, and his proofs of manliness for the Grevilles.

The Gibraltar man did not come on Saturday; and Miss Fosbrook had been the saving of several stamps by sending some queer little letters in her own to Mrs. Merrifield, so that on Monday morning the hoard was increased to seven-and-sixpence; although between fines and "couldn't helps," Henry's sixpence had melted down to a halfpenny, which "was not worth while."

On this day arrived a servant from the Park, bringing a delicate little lilac envelope, stamped with a tiny rose, and directed to Miss Merrifield. There was another rose on the top of the lilac paper; and the writing was in a very neat hand.

My dear Susan,

Mamma desires me to say that she hopes you and Bessie and Annie will come to dine early to-morrow, and play with me, and that Miss Fosbury will come with you. She hopes your Mamma is better, and would be glad to have her address in London.

I am your affectionate
IDA ARABELLA GREVILLE.

"Oh! Miss Fosbrook, may we go?" cried the girls with sparkling eyes.

Mrs. Merrifield had written that one or two such invitations might be accepted, but she had rather it did not happen too often, as visits at the Park were unsettling to some of the children. So as this was the first, Christabel gladly consented, rather curious and rather shy on her own account.

Elizabeth begged for the rose, to copy it, and as there were no little ones present to seize it, she was allowed to have it; while Susan groaned and sighed over the misfortune of having to write a "horrible note" just at play-time; and the boys treated it as a sort of insult to the whole family that Ida should have mistaken their governess's name.

"Tell her you won't go till she has it right," said Sam; at which Annie made a vehement outcry of "No, no!" such as made them all laugh at her thinking him in earnest.

Susan's note began -

My dear Ida,

We shuold -

But then perceiving that something was the matter with
her word, Susan sat and looked at it, till at last,
perceiving that her u and o had changed places, she
tried putting a top to the u, and made it like an a; while
the filling up the o made it become a blot, such as
caught Bessie's eye.

"O Susie, you won't send such a thing as that up
to Ida?"

"No - that WOULD be a 'horrible note,'" said her
governess; and she ruled the lines again.

"Dear me," said Susan impatiently; "can't one send a
message up by the man that we'll all come, without
this fuss?"

But Miss Fosbrook said that would be very uncivil;
and Susan, groaning, stretched every finger till the
lines were finished, and began again, in her scraggy
round-hand - getting safely through the "should," and
also through "like to come very much;" but when Miss
Fosbrook looked up next, she saw that the rest of the
note consisted of -

Mamma is at Grandmamma's, No. 12, St., Grovensor
Place.

I am your affectionate
SUSANNA MERRIFIELD.

"My dear, I am very sorry."

"What! won't that do?" sighed Susan, beginning to get into despair.

Miss Fosbrook pointed to the word "Grovensor."

"Oh dear! oh dear! I thought I had got that tiresome word this time. Why can't it put its ss and ns into their proper sensible places?" cried poor Susan, to whom it was a terrible enemy. She used to try them in different places all the way round, in hopes that one might at last be right.

"Can't you remember what I told you, that the first Grosvenor was the grand huntsman? Grosveneur in French; that would show you where to put the s - gros, great."

But Susan never wished to remember anything French; and Sam observed that "the man deserved to be spelt wrong if he called himself by a French name. Why couldn't he be content to be Mr. Grandhunter?"

"But as he is not, we must spell his name right, or Mrs. Greville will be shocked," said Miss Fosbrook.

"Please can't you scratch it out?" said the disconsolate Susan.

"*I* should not like to send a note with a scratch in it. Besides, yours is hardly civil."

"No, indeed," said Elizabeth; "don't you know how people answer invitations, Susie? I'll tell you. 'Miss Susanna, and Miss Elizabeth, and Miss Annie Merrifield will be very happy to do the honour of dining with - ' Sam, why do you laugh at me always?"

"Why, you are telling Ida you will do her honour by dining with her."

"People always do honour when they dine," said Elizabeth. "I know they do."

"They profess to receive the honour, not confer it, Bessie," said Miss Fosbrook, laughing; "but I don't think that is the model for Susie's note. It would be as much too formal as hers was too blunt."

"Must I do it again?" said Susan. "I had rather not go, if it is to be such a plague."

"Indeed, I fear you must, Susie. It is quite needful to learn how to write a respectable note; really a more difficult thing than writing a long letter. I am sorry for you; but if you were not so careless in your letters to Mamma this would come more easily to you."

But this time Miss Fosbrook not only ruled another sheet, but wrote, in fair large-hand on a slate, the words, that Susan might copy them without fresh troubles:

We are much obliged to your Mamma for her kind invitation, and shall have much pleasure in coming with Miss Fosbrook to dine with you and spend the day. I am sorry to say that Mamma was not quite so well when last we heard. Her address is - No. 12, - St., Grosvenor-place.

Susan thought that here were a very serious number of words, and begged hard for leave to leave out her sorrow. Of course she was sorry, but what was the use of telling Ida so?

Miss Fosbrook thought it looked better, but Susan might do as she pleased.

"I wouldn't say it, then," said Sam. "I wouldn't say it only to look better to Ida." With which words he and Hal walked off to the garden.

Would it be believed? Susan, in her delight at being near the end, forgot the grand huntsman, and made the unlucky Place "Grovesnor," and then, in her haste to mend it, put her finger into the wet ink, and smeared not only that word, but all the line above!

It was a shame and a wonder that a girl of her age should be so incapable of producing a creditable note; and Miss Fosbrook was very near scolding her but she had pity on the tearful eyes and weary fingers, and spoke cheerfully: "There, that was almost the thing. One more trial, Susan, and you need never be afraid of Ida's notes again."

If Susan could not write notes, at least she was not cross; and it would be well if many who could send off a much better performance with far less difficulty could go to work as patiently as she did, without one pettish word to Miss Fosbrook, though that lady seemed to poor Susie as hard a task mistress as if she could have helped it. This time Miss Fosbrook authorized the leaving out of the spending the day, and suggested that S. would be enough without the whole Susanna, and she mercifully directed the cover to Miss Greville.

"There, my dear, you have worked hard for your pleasure," she said, as Susan extended each hand to its broadest stretch to uncramp them, and stretched herself backwards as if she wanted to double her head down to her heels. "I shall give you a good mark, Susie, as if it had been a lesson."

Susan deserved it, for her patient perseverance had been all out of obedience, not in the mere desire of having her note admired. Indeed, good child, at the best it was a very poor affair for a girl of twelve, and Miss Fosbrook was ashamed of it when she looked at Ida's lady-like little billet.

"But I wonder," said she to herself, "whether I shall feel as if I would change my dear stupid Susan for Miss Ida?"

Meanwhile Susan flew screaming and leaping out into the garden in a mad tom-boy fashion; but that could well be pardoned, as there were only her sisters to see her; and the pleasure of having persevered and done her best was enough to make her heart and her limbs dance for merriment.

Depend upon it, however wretched and miserable hard application to what we do not like may seem at the moment, it is the only way to make play-times really delicious.

CHAPTER IX.

Miss Fosbrook soon knew what Mrs. Merrifield meant by saying that visits at the Park unsettled the children. Susan indeed, though liking anything that shortened lessons by an hour, and made a change, was not so fond of being on her good behaviour at the Park as to be greatly exalted at the prospect; but Elizabeth and Annie were changed beings. They were constantly breaking out with some new variety of wonder. They wondered whether they should dine in the school-room, or at Mrs. Greville's luncheon; they wondered if Mr. Greville would speak to them; they wondered whether Fraulein Munsterthal would be cross; they wondered if Ida still played with dolls; and they looked as if they thought themselves wonderful, too, for going out for a day!

Nay, the wonders were at their tongues' end even when lessons began, and put their farthings in great peril; and when they had nothing else to wonder at, they wondered when it would be twelve o'clock, and took no pains to swallow enormous yawns. Once, over her copy, Elizabeth exclaimed, "Now! yes, this is necessary, Miss Fosbrook! May not we wear our white frocks?"

"They are not ironed," answered Susan.

"Oh, do let me go and tell Mary! There's lots of time," said Bessie, who had lately thought it cruel of the clock to point only to half-past ten, and never bethought herself how Mary would like to be called off from her scrubbing to iron three white frocks.

"Would your Mamma wish it?" asked Christabel.

"Oh dear no," was Susan's answer; "we always wear clean ones of our every-day frocks. Our white ones are only for dinner-parties and Christmas-trees."

Bessie grumbled. "How cross! I hate those nasty old spotty cottons;" and Johnnie returned to the old story - "Little vain pussy-cat."

Up went Miss Fosbrook's warning pencil, she shook her head, and held out her hand for two fines. Elizabeth began to gulp and sob.

"Oh, don't, Betty!" cried Susan. "Stop while you can. You won't like going up with red eyes. There, I'll pay your fine; and there's another for my speaking."

"No, Susie; that was not foolish speaking, but kind words," said Miss Fosbrook; "but no more now; go on, Annie."

But Annie, who was reading a little history of St. Paul, would call Cilicia, Cicilia, and when told to spell it she began to cry too decidedly for Susan's good-nature to check her tears. And not only did Elizabeth's copy look as if she had written it with claws instead of fingers, but she was grieving over her spotted cotton instead of really seeking for places in her map. Thus the Moselle obstinately hid itself; and she absolutely shed tears because Miss Fosbrook declared that Frankfort WAS on the Maine. For the first time she had her grammar turned back upon her hands. How many mistakes Annie made would be really past telling; for these two little girls had their whole minds quite upset by the thought of a day's pleasure; and as they never tried to restrain themselves, and to "be sober, be vigilant," they gave way before all the little trials in their paths-were first careless, and then fractious. Perhaps when they were older they would find out that this uplifted sense of excited expectation is the very warning to be heedful.

If Miss Fosbrook had been a strict governess, she would have told them they did not deserve to go at all; or at any rate, that Bessie must repeat her grammar better, and re-write her copy, and that Annie's unlucky addition sum must be made to prove; but she had seen her little sisters nearly as bad in prospect of a pantomime, so she was merciful, and sent them in good time to brush their hair, put on their spotted cottons, and wash off as much as possible of the red mottling left by those foolish tears.

Their spirits rose again as fast as they had sunk; and it was a lively walk through the park to the great house, with a good deal of skipping and jumping at first, and then, near the door, a little awe and gravity.

They were taken through a side-door of the hall to the school-room, where Ida and her governess received them. It was the first time that Christabel had seen her out of her beplumed hat, and she thought her a pleasant, bright-looking little girl, not at all set up or conceited. Her mauve muslin, flounced though it was up to her waist, showed that it had been wise to

Charlotte M. Yonge

withstand Bessie's desire for the white muslins; but
Miss Fosbrook had enough to do on her own account
with the endeavour to understand the German governess's foreign accent, without attending to the children
more than was necessary.

It was not a very remarkable day, and the pleasures of
it seemed hardly enough to justify the little girls' great
excitement. There was first the dinner at the luncheon
of the parents, where the children sat up rather formal
and subdued, and not quite certain what all the dishes
might contain, a little afraid of getting what they
COULD not eat, though desirous of making experi-
ments in this land of wonders. None of them had
forgotten, and they thought no one else had, how
Bessie had once come to disgrace by bursting out
crying over the impossibility of finishing some terrible
rice-bordered greenish yellow stuff that burnt her
mouth beyond bearing, and which Ida called curry, and
said people in the East Indies liked. However, that was
when Bessie had been a very little girl; and she still
continued adventurous, saying, "Yes, if you please," to
cutlets set round in a wreath, with all their bones
sticking up, and covered with a reddish incrustation
that Susan and Annie thought so unnatural, that they
preferred the boiled chicken that at least they could
understand, though it had funny-hooking accompani-
ments in the sauce. And Hal's report of some savoury
jelly which he had once encountered would have
deterred them from the pink transparency in the shape
of a shell, if they had not seen Bessie getting on very
well with it, Miss Fosbrook happily perceiving and
cutting short Annie's intended inquiry whether it were
nice. To her great relief, this was the only want of
manners betrayed by her little savages, and she was
able to keep her attention tolerably free from them, so

as to look at the pictures on the walls, observe the two boys, Hal's friends, and talk to Mrs. Greville, who made conversation with her very pleasantly.

She was much grieved to perceive, from what that lady said, that Mrs. Merrifield was thought to be much more ill, and in a far more alarming state, than she had at all understood. The girls were too young to enter into the tone of sad sympathy with which Mrs. Greville spoke, and the manner in which a doubt was expressed whether the Captain would be able to sail with Admiral Penrose if he should have the offer; and as soon as she saw that they and their governess were in ignorance, she turned it off; but she had said enough to fill Christabel with anxiety and desire to know more; and as soon as the dinner was over, and the little girls had run off together to visit Ida's beautiful cockatoo in the conservatory, she turned to Fraulein Munsterthal, and begged to hear whether she knew more than had been said.

Fraulein Munsterthal did not quite know that such a person as Mrs. Merrifield was in existence; but she was very amiable and warm-hearted, and said how sad it was to think of the trouble that hung over "these so careless children," and was doubly kind to the girls when they came back from their conversation with pretty "Cocky," who set up his lemon-coloured crest, coughed, sneezed, and said "Cocky want a biscuit!" to admiration, till the boys were seen approaching; when Ida, knowing that some torment would follow, took herself and her visitors back to the protection of the governesses in time to prevent the cockatoo from being made to fly at the girls, and powder them with the white dust under his feathers.

Charlotte M. Yonge

The afternoon was spent in the garden, the little girls betaking themselves to a pretty moss-covered arbour, where there was a grand doll's feast. Ida had no less than twenty-three dolls, ranging from the magnificent Rosalind, who had real hair that could be brushed, and was as large as little Sally at home, down to poor little china Mildred, whose proper dwelling-place was a bath, and who had with great difficulty been put into petticoats enough to make her fit to be seen out of it. Now nobody at home could have saved the life of a doll for a single day, and Susan and Elizabeth were both thought far above them; but these beautifully arrayed young ladies had always been the admiration of the heart of Bessie as well as of Annie, and they were not too old for extreme satisfaction in handling their elegant ladyships, and still more their beautiful dinner and tea-service of pink and white ware.

Susan, though she could not write a note, or do lessons like Ida, was older in the ways of life, and played rather as she did with the little ones at home than for her own amusement. She would much rather have had the fun of "cats and mice" with her brothers; and but for the honour of the thing, so perhaps would Annie. However, they were all very happy, getting the dolls up in the morning, giving Mildred washing enough for all the twenty-three, making them breakfast, hearing lessons, in which Ida was governess, and made them talk so many languages that Annie was alarmed. Of course one of the young ladies was very naughty, and was treated with extreme severity; then there was dinner, a walk, an illness, and a dinner-party. While all the time the two real governesses sat in the shade outside, and talked in English or German as best they might, the Fraulein understanding Christabel's English the best, as did Christabel the Fraulein's German. They began to make friends, and to wish to see more of one another.

There was a walk round the garden, and admiration of the beautiful flowers, and the fountain and pond of gold-fish, till the boys came home, and got hold of the garden-engine for watering, crying out, "Fire! fire!" and squirting out the showers of water very much in the direction of the girls.

Ida became quite crimson red, and got hold of Susan's hand to drag her away; then, as the foremost drops of another shower touched her, she faced about, and said, "Osmond! don't, or I'll tell Mamma." There was a great rude laugh, as of boys who well knew the threat was never put in execution; and poor Fraulein Munsterthal only shook her head at Miss Fosbrook's look of amaze, and said in German that "die Knaben" were far too unartig for her to keep in order. She pitied Miss Fosbrook for having so many in charge as to destroy all peace. And if Sam and Hal had been like these two, Christabel felt that she could have done nothing with them. To her dismay, Osmond and Martin came in to the school-room tea; and she never had thought to feel so thankful for poor dear Susan's slowness of comprehension, for, from their whispers among themselves, and from their poor tormented sister's blushes, she was clear that the "fire" was a piece of bad wit on Susan's red hair. Boys who could so basely insult a guest, and that a girl, she was sure must be bad companions for Sam and Henry. Such little gentlemen as they had been at dinner too, so polite and well-behaved before their father and mother! There could be no doubt that something must be very wrong about them, or they would not change so entirely when out of sight. It is not always true that a child must be deceitful who is less good in the absence of the authorities; because their presence is a help and a restraint, checking the beginning of mischief, and removing temptation; but one who does not fall by weakness, but intentionally alters his conduct the instant the elder is gone, shows that his will has been disobedient all along

By and by Mr. Greville's voice was heard calling, "Martin! Osmond!" As they went out to meet him in the passage, Miss Fosbrook clearly overheard, "Here is the spring of the garden-engine spoilt. Do you know anything about it?"

"No."

"You have not been meddling with it?"

"No." And they ran downstairs.

The colour flushed into Christabel's cheeks with horror. She was glad that her little girls were all in Ida's room, listening to a musical-box, and well out of hearing of such fearfully direct falsehoods, as it seemed to her, not knowing that the boys excused it to their own minds by the notion that it was not the SPRING of the engine that they had been meddling with, and that so they did not know how the harm had been done - as if it made it any better that they lied to themselves as well as their father! The German saw her dismay, and began to say how unlike her Ida was to her brothers - so truthful, so gentle, and courteous; but poor Christabel could not get over the thought of the ease and readiness with which deceit came to these boys. Could their daily companions, Samuel and Henry, have learnt the same effrontery, and be deceiving her all this time? No, no, she could not, would not think it! Assuredly not of Sam! She was very glad not to see the boys again, and went home with her pupils, rather heavy-hearted, at eight o'clock, just as Ida was to put on her white muslin and pink ribbons, and go down after dinner for half an hour.

There were many kisses at parting, and a whole box of sweets, done up in beautifully coloured and gold and silver paper, presented to the little visitors; but it might be supposed that the girls were tired, for there was a fretful snarling all the way across the park, because Elizabeth insisted that the gifts should be called bon-bons, and the others would hear of nothing but goodies. Nobody looked at the beautiful evening sky, nor at the round red moon coming up like a lamp behind the trees, nor at the first stars peeping out, nor even at the green light of the glow-worm - all which were more beautiful than anything Ida had shown them, except perhaps the hothouse flowers; and at last two such cross ill-tempered voices sounded from Bessie and Annie, that Christabel turned round and declared that she should not let the sugar-plums be touched for a week if another word were said about them.

She hoped that when the visit was over it would be done with; but no such thing. Though Susan was her own good hearty self, Elizabeth had not recovered either on that day of the next from the effects of the pleasuring. On each she cried over her lessons, and was cross at whatever the boys said to her, made a fuss about keeping the ornamental cases of the bon-bons, and went about round-backed, peevish, and discontented, finding everything flat and ugly after her one peep at the luxuries of the Park. Her farthings melted away fast; but she seemed to think this her misfortune, not her fault. She did not try to talk to Miss Fosbrook, feeling perhaps that she was in a naughty mood, which she would not try to shake off; and she made no attempt to go on with her present for her Mamma, it looked so poor and trumpery after the beautiful things she had seen.

Nor did Christabel like to remind her of it, fearing that the occasion for giving it might never come; but she did feel that it was a mournful thing to see the child, who was in danger of so fearful a sorrow, wasting her grief in pining after foolish fancies, and turning what should have been a refreshing holiday into an occasion of longing after what she thus made into pomps and vanities of this wicked world. Christabel had heard that people who murmur among blessings often have those blessings snatched away, and this made her tremble for poor little discontented Elizabeth.

CHAPTER X.

"There!" exclaimed Susan, "I really have got a letter from Papa himself. What a prize!"

"You'll have to mind your Grosvenor when you answer HIM," said Sam; "but hollo, what's the matter?"

For Susan's eyes had grown large, and her whole face scarlet, and she gave a little cry as she read.

"Your Mamma, my dear?" asked Miss Fosbrook.

"Oh, Mamma - Mamma is so very ill!" and Susan throw the letter down, and broke into a fit of sobbing.

Sam caught it up, and Elizabeth came to read it with him, both standing still and not speaking a word, but staring at the letter with their eyes fixed.

"What is it, my dear?" said Miss Fosbrook, tenderly putting her arm round Susan; but she sobbed too much to make a word distinct, and Bessie held out the letter to her governess, looking white, and too much awed to speak.

Captain Merrifield wrote in short, plain, sad words, that he thought it right that his children should know how matters stood. The doctors' treatment, for which

Charlotte M. Yonge

their mother had been taken to London, had not succeeded, but had occasioned such terrible illness, that unless by the mercy of God she became much better in the course of a day or two, she could not live. If she should be worse, he would either write or telegraph, and Susan and Sam must be ready to set out at once on the receipt of such a message, and come up by the next train to London, where they should be met at the station. He had promised their mother that in case of need he would send for them.

God bless you, my poor children, and have mercy on us all!

Your loving father,
H. MERRIFIELD.

That was all; and Christabel felt, more than even the children did, from how full and heavy a heart those words had been written.

Though she hardly knew how to speak, she tried to comfort Susan by showing her that her father had evidently not given up all hope; but Susan was crying more at the thought of her Mamma's present illness and pain than with fear of the future; and Sam said sadly, "He would not have written at all unless it had been very bad indeed."

"Yes," said Miss Fosbrook; "but I believe, in cases like this, there is often great fear, and then very speedy improvement."

"Oh dear," said Bessie, speaking for the first time, "I know it will be. Little girls in story-books always do have their mammas - die!"

"Story-books are all nonsense, so it won't happen," said Sam; and really it seemed as if the habit of contradicting Bessie had suggested to him the greatest consolation that had yet occurred.

Just then Henry and the younger ones came in, and learnt the tidings. Henry wept as bitterly as his elder sister, and John and Annie both did the same; but David did not speak one word, as if he hardly took in what was the matter, and, going to the window, took up his lesson-books as usual.

"It is nine o'clock, Hal," said Sam presently.

"Oh, we can't go to Mr. Carey to-day," said Hal.

"Yes, we shall," returned Sam.

"Oh don't," cried Susan. "Suppose a telegraph should come!"

"Well, then you can send for me," said Sam. "Come, Hal."

"How can you, Sam?" said Henry crossly; "I know Mr. Carey will give us leave when he knows."

"I don't want leave," said Sam; "I don't want to kick up a row, as you'll do if you stay at home."

"Well then, if the message comes, I shall take Susie to London instead of you. I'm sure they want me most!"

"No, go down to Mr. Carey's with your brother, if you please, Hal," said Miss Fosbrook decidedly. "If he should tell you not to stay, I can't help it; but you will

Charlotte M. Yonge

none of you do any good by hanging about without doing your daily duties."

Hal saw he had no chance, and marched off, muttering about its being very hard. Sam picked up his books, and turned to go, with a grave steady look that was quite manly in its sadness, only stopping to say, "Now, Jackie, you be good! - Please Miss Fosbrook, let him run down after me if the message comes, and I'll be back before the horse is out."

Miss Fosbrook promised, and could not help shaking hands with the brave boy, if only to show that she felt with him.

"Then must we all do our lessons?" asked Annie disconsolately, when he was gone.

"Yes, my dear; I think we shall all be the better for not neglecting what we ought to do. But there is one thing that we can do for your dear Mamma; you know what I mean. Suppose you each went away alone for five minutes, and were to come back when I ring the little bell?"

The first to come back was Annie, with the question in a low whisper, "Miss Fosbrook, will God make Mamma better if we are very good?"

Miss Fosbrook kissed her, saying, "My dear little girl, I cannot tell. All I can certainly tell you is, that He hears the prayers of good children, and if it be better for her and for you He will give her back to you."

Annie did not quite understand, but she entered into what Miss Fosbrook said enough to wish to be good;

so she took up her book, and began to learn with all her might.

Elizabeth would have thought it much more like a little girl in a book to have done no lessons, but have sat thinking, and perhaps reading the Bible all day; but on the whole Elizabeth had hardly thoughts enough to last her so long; nor was she deep or serious enough to have done herself much good by keeping the Bible open before her. In fact she did lose her verse in merely reading the chapter for the day! So it was just as well that she had something to do that was not play, and that was a duty, and thus might give the desire to be good something to bear upon.

But Christabel saw by Susan's face, and heard in the shaken voice with which she took her turn in the reading, that she could not have given her mind to her tasks, and did not need them to keep her out of mischief. It would have been cruel to have required her to sit down to them just then, and her governess was glad to be able to excuse her on account of the packing-up. All her things and Sam's must be got ready in case of an immediate start, and she was sent up to the nursery to take care of the little ones, while Nurse and Mary mended, ironed, and packed.

To be sure Nurse Freeman made poor Susan unnecessarily unhappy by being sure that it was all the fault of the London doctors; but she was a kind, tender old woman, and her petting was a great comfort to the poor girl. What did her most good, however, was sitting quite quiet with the little ones while they were asleep, and all alone; it seemed to rest and compose her, and she always loved to be in charge of them. Poor child! she might soon have to be their little mother! She was able to play with them when they awoke, and cheered herself up with their pretty ways, and by finding how quickly Baby was learning to walk. Ah! but would Mamma ever see her walk?

If any of the children thought it unjust that Susan's lessons should be let off, they were wrong. Parents and teachers must have the power of doing such things without being judged. Sometimes they see that a child is really unable to learn, when the others perceive no difference; and it would be very harsh and cruel to oppress one who is out of order for fear little silly, idle, healthy things should think themselves hardly used.

At any rate, the lessons were capitally done; and when the children met again, they were all so much brighter and more hopeful, that they quite believed that their Mamma was going to get better very fast. Bessie especially was so resolved that thus it should be, that she shut herself into Miss Fosbrook's room, and drew and painted with all her might, as if preparing for Mamma's birthday made it certain that it would be kept.

The boys brought word that they would have a holiday the next day, as it was the Feast of St. Barnabas, and after morning service Mr. Carey was going to meet his brother and bring him home.

"I shall be all the more certain to get the sovereign, or two sovereigns," said Henry to David, the only person whom he could find to listen to him, "if Sam is gone; and everyone will be caring about me."

"And then you'll give it to the pig," said David.

"Oh yes, to be sure. You will grow into a pig yourself if you go on that way, David."

However, David, partaking the family distrust of Hal's birds-in-the-bush, and being started on the subject of the hoard, ran up to Sam, who was learning his lessons by way of something to do, and said, "If you go to London, Sam, may I have your sixpence on Monday for the pig?"

"I don't know that I am going."

"But if you do - or we sha'n't get the pig."

"I don't care."

"Don't you care if we don't get the pig?"

"No. Be off with you."

David next betook himself to his eldest sister, who was trying to write to her father, and finding such a letter harder and sadder work than that to Ida Greville, though no one teased her about writing, blots, or spelling.

"If you go to London, Susie," said he, in the very same words, "may I have your sixpence on Monday for the pig?"

"Oh, Davie, don't be tiresome!"

David only said it over again in the same words, and put his hand down on her letter in his earnestness.

"Come away, Davie," said Miss Fosbrook; "don't tease

your sister."

"I want her to say I may have her sixpence on Monday for the pig."

"No, you sha'n't, then," said Susan angrily; "you care for the nasty pig more than for poor Mamma or anyone else, and you sha'n't have it."

So seldom did Susan say anything cross, that everyone looked up surprised. Miss Fosbrook saw that it was sheer unhappiness that made her speak sharply, and would not take any notice, except by gently taking away the pertinacious David.

He was very much distressed at the refusal; and when Miss Fosbrook told him that his brother and sister could not think of such things when they were in such trouble, he only answered, "But Hannah Higgins won't get her pig."

Miss Fosbrook was vexed herself that her friend David should seem possessed with this single idea, as if it shut out all others from his mind. He was consoled fast enough; for Susan, with another great sob, threw down her pen, and coming up to stroke him down with her inky fingers, cried out, "O Davie, Davie, I didn't mean it; I don't know why I said it. You shall have my sixpence, or anything! But, oh dear, I wish the message was come, and we were going to dear Mamma, for I can't write, and I don't know what to do."

Then she went back to her place, and tried to write, and sat with her head on her hand, and dawdled and cried and blotted till it grew so near post-time that at last Miss Fosbrook took the longest of her scrawls, and writing three lines at the bottom to say how it was with them all, directed it to Captain Merrifield, thinking that he would like it better than nothing from home, sent it off, and made Susan come out to refresh her hot eyes and burning head in the garden.

Sam presently came and walked on her other side, gravely and in silence, glad to be away from the chatter and disputes of the younger ones. That summons had made them both feel older, and less like children, than ever before; but they did not speak much, only, when they sat down on a garden bench, as Miss Fosbrook held Susan's hand, she presently found some rough hard young fingers stealing into her own on the other side, and saw Sam's eyes glistening with unshed tears. She stroked his hand, and they dropped fast: but he was ashamed to cry, and quickly dried them.

"I think," she said, "that you will be a man, Sam; take care of Susan, and be a comfort to your father."

"I hope I shall," said Sam; "but I don't know how."

"Nobody can tell how beforehand," she said. "Only watch to see what he may seem to want to have done for him. Sit quietly by, and don't get in the way."

"Were you ever so unhappy, Miss Fosbrook?" asked Susan.

"Yes, once I was, when my father was knocked down by an omnibus, and was very ill."

"Tell us about it?" said Susan.

She did tell them of her week of sorrow and anxious

care of the younger children, and the brightening ray of hope at last. It seemed to freshen both up, and give them hopes, for each drew a long sigh of relief; and then Sam said, "Papa wrote to Mr. Carey. She is to be prayed for in church to-morrow."

"Oh," said Susan, with a sound as of dismay, which made Christabel ask in wonder why she was sorry, when, from Susan's half-uttered words, she found that the little girl fancied that a "happy issue out of all her afflictions" meant death.

"Oh no, my dear," she said. "What it means is, that the afflictions may end happily in whatever way God may see to be best; it may be in getting well; it may be the other way: at any rate, it is asking that the distress may be over, not saying how."

"Isn't there some other prayer in the Prayer-book about it?" said Sam, looking straight before him.

"I will show you where to find it, in the Visitation of the Sick. I dare say it has often been read to her."

The boy and girl came in with her, and brought their Prayer-books to her room, that she might mark them.

This had been a strange, long, sad day of waiting and watching for the telegram, and the children even fancied it might come in the middle of the night; but Miss Fosbrook thought this unlikely, and looked for the morrow's post. There was no letter. It was very disappointing, but Miss Fosbrook thought it a good sign, since at least the danger could not be more pressing, and delay always left room for hope.

The children readily believed her; they were too young to go on dwelling long on what was not in sight; and even Susan was cheerful, and able to think about other things after her night's rest, and the relief of not hearing a worse account.

The children might do as they pleased about going to church on saints' days, and on this day all the three girls wished to go, as soon as it had been made clear that even if the message should come before the short service would be over, there would be ample time to reach the station before the next train. Miss Fosbrook was glad to prove this, for not only did she wish to have them in church, but she thought the weary watching for the telegram was the worst thing possible for Susan. Sam was also going to church, but Henry hung back, after accompanying them to the end of the kitchen-garden. "I wouldn't go, Sam; just suppose if the message came without anyone at home, and you had to set out at once!"

"We couldn't," said Sam; "there's no train."

"Oh, but they always put on a special train whenever anyone is ill."

"Then there would be plenty!"

"At least they did when Mr. Greville's mother was ill, so they will now; and then you may ride upon the engine, for there won't be any carriages, you know. I say, Sam, if you go to church, and the telegraph comes, I shall set off."

"You'll do no such thing," said Sam. "You had much better come to church."

"No, I sha'n't. It is like a girl to go to church on a week-day."

"It is much more like a girl to mind what a couple of asses, like the Grevilles, say," returned Sam, taking up his cap and running after his sisters and their governess.

"It is quite right," observed Henry to John and David, who alone remained to listen to him, "that one of us should stay in case the telegraph comes in, and there are any orders to give. I can catch the pony, you know, and ride off to Bonchamp, and if the special train is there, I shall get upon the engine."

"But it is Sam and Susan who are going."

"Oh, that's only because Sam is eldest. I know Mamma would like to have me much better, because I don't walk hard like Sam; and when I get there, she will be so much better already, and we shall be all right; and Admiral Penrose will be so delighted at my courage in riding on the engine and putting out the explosion, or something, that he will give me my appointment as naval cadet at once, and I shall have a dirk and a uniform, and a chest of my own, and be an officer, and get promoted for firing red-hot shot out of the batteries at Gibraltar."

"Master Hal!" exclaimed Purday, "don't throw them little apples about."

"They are red-hot shot, Purday!"

"I'll red-hot shot you if you break my cucumber frames, young gentleman! Come, get out with you."

Probably anxiety made Purday cross as well as everyone else, or else he distrusted Henry's discretion without Sam, for he hunted the little boys away wherever they went. Now they would break the cucumber frames; now they would meddle with the gooseberries, or trample on the beds; and at last he only relented so far as to let David stay with him on condition of being very good, and holding the little cabbages as he planted them out.

"Master Davie was a solemn one," Purday said, and they were great friends; but Hal and Johnnie were fairly turned out, as their idle hands were continually finding fresh mischief to do in their sauntering desultory mood.

"I think," said Hal, "since Purday is so savage, we'll go and look out at the gate, and then we shall see if the telegraph comes."

Johnnie had no clear idea what a telegraph was, and was curious to know how it would come, rather expecting it to be a man in a red coat on horseback, blowing a horn - a sight that certainly was not to be missed; so he willingly strolled down after Henry to the gate leading to the lane.

"I can't see any way at all," said Henry, looking out into the lane. "I shall get up, and so see over into the bend of the road;" and Hal mounted to the topmost bar of the gate, and sat astride there, John scrambling after him not quite so easily, his legs being less long, and his dress less convenient. Both knew that their Papa strongly objected to their climbing on this iron gate, the newest and handsomest thing about the place; but thought Hal, "Of course no one will care what I do when I am so anxious about poor Mamma!" and thought Johnnie, "What Hal does, of course I may do!"

So there the two young gentlemen sat perched, each with one leg on either side of the new iron gate. It was rather like sitting on the edge of a knife; and John could scarcely reach his toes down to rest them on the bar below, but he held on by the spikes, and it was so new and glorious a position, that it made up for a good deal to be five feet above the road; moreover, Hal said it was just like the mast-head of a man-of-war - at LEAST, when the waves didn't dash right overhead, like the picture of the Eddystone Lighthouse.

"Hollo! what, a couple of cherubs aloft!" cried a voice from the road; and looking round, Henry beheld the two Grevilles.

"Yes," he answered; "it's very jolly up here."

"Eh! is it? Riding on a razor, to my mind. Come down, and have a lark," said Osmond; while Martin, undoing the gate, proceeded to swing it backwards and forwards, to John's extreme terror; but the more he clung to the spikes, and cried for mercy, the quicker Martin swung it, shouting with laughter at his fright. Henry meanwhile scrambled and tumbled to the ground, and caught the gate and held it fast, while he asked what his friends had been about. One held up a scarlet flask of powder, the other a bag of shot.

"You haven't got a gun!"

"No, but we know where gardener keeps his; and the governor's out for the day. Come along, Hal: you shall have your turn."

"I don't want to go far from home to-day."

"Oh, stuff! What was it Mamma heard, Osmond? That your mother was ever so much better, wasn't it?"

"I thought it was worse," said Osmond.

"Well, never mind: your hanging about here won't do her any good, I suppose."

"No; but -"

"Oh, he'll catch it from the governess! - I say, how many seams shall you have to sew to-day, Hal?"

"I don't sew seams: I do as I please."

"Ha! Is that them coming out of church!"

"Oh, it is! it is!" cried John from his elevation. "Oh, help me down, Hal!"

But Henry did not want Miss Fosbrook to find him partaking in gate-climbing; and either that desire, or the general terror a bad conscience, made him and the Grevilles run helter-skelter the opposite way, leaving poor little John stuck on the top of the gate, quite giddy at the thought of coming down alone, and almost as much afraid of being there caught by Miss Fosbrook coming home from church.

It was a false alarm after all, that the congregation were coming out. John would have been glad if they had; for nothing could be more miserable than sitting up there, his fingers tired of clutching the spikes, his feet strained with reaching down to the bar, his legs chilled with the wind, his head almost giddy when he thought of climbing down. He would have cried, could he have spared a hand to rub his eyes with; he had a great mind to have roared for help, especially when he heard feet upon the road; but these turned out to belong to five little village boys, still smaller than himself, who, when they saw the young gentleman on his perch, all stood still in a row, with their mouths wide open, staring at him. Johnnie scorned to let them think he was not riding there for his own pleasure; so he tried to put a bold face of the matter, and look as much at ease and indifferent as he could, under great bodily fear and discomfort, the injury of his brother's desertion, the expectation of disgrace, and the reflection that he was being disobedient to his parents in the height of their trouble!

There is nothing in grief that of necessity makes children or grown people good. Sometimes, especially when there is suspense, it fills them with excitement, as well as putting them out of their usual habits; and thus it often happens that there are tremendous explosions of naughtiness just when some one is ill in a house, and the children ought to be most good. But it is certain that unless trouble be taken in the right way, it makes people worse instead of better

CHAPTER XI.

Hal had got into a mood in which he was tired of fears and of waiting for tidings, and was glad to shake off the thought, and be carried along to something new, he and the Grevilles were rather fond of one another's company, in an idle sort of way. They "put him up to things," as he said; they made a variety; and he was always glad of listeners to his wonderful stories, which rather diverted the other boys, who, though they sometimes made game of them, were much less apt to pick them to pieces than was Sam.

Poor Captain Merrifield! what had not befallen him, according to his son? He had been stuck on to a rock of loadstone; he had been bitten by mosquitos as big as jackdaws - at least as jack-snipes; he had sat down to rest on the trunk of a fallen tree, and it whisked him over on his face, and turned out to he a rattle-snake - at least, a boa-constrictor! Nay, Henry discoursed on the ponies he had himself tamed, the rabbits he had shot, the trees he had climbed, the nests he had found, the rats he had killed, in terms he durst not use when his brother was by; or if he did, and Sam brought him to book, he always said "it was all fun." It often seemed as if he did not himself know whether he meant to be believed or otherwise; and as to his intentions for his sailor life, they were, as has been already seen, of the most splendid character! Sometimes he shot the French

Charlotte M. Yonge

admiral dead from the mast-head; sometimes he sailed into Plymouth with the whole enemy's fleet behind him; sometimes he, the youngest midshipman, rescued the whole crew in a wreck where all the other officers were drowned; sometimes he shot a shark through the head, just as it was about to make a meal of Prince Alfred!

He certainly was thus an entertaining companion to those who did not pay heed to truth, and liked to hear or laugh at great swelling words; and the Grevilles, on their idle day, were glad to have him with them, and were rather curious to prove how much fact there was in his boast of being a most admirable shot.

Meddling with guns was absolutely forbidden to all the three, except by special permission and with an elder looking on; but the Grevilles were not in the habit of obeying, except when they were forced to do so; and Henry, having once begun to think no one would heed his present doings, was ready to go on rather than be accused of minding his governess.

So the gardener's gun was taken from the hiding-place, whither it had been conveyed from the tool-house; and the three boys ran off together, their first object being to get out of the Greville grounds, where they could be met by any of the men. They got quite out into the fields, before they ventured to stop that Osmond might load the gun. Each was to take a shot in turn; Osmond tried first, at a poor innocent young thrush, newly come out for his earliest flight. Happily he missed it; Martin claimed the next, and for want of anything better to shoot, took aim at the scare-crow in the middle of Farmer Grice's beans. He was sure that he had hit it, and showed triumphantly the great holes in its hat; but the other boys were strongly persuaded that they had been there before.

"Well, come away," said Osmond; "this is a great deal too near old Grice's farm-yard. If we go popping about here, we shall have him out upon us, for an old tiger as he is!"

"Come along, then," said Martin.

But Hal had just got the gun, and saw something so black and shiny through the hedge, that he was persuaded that a flock of rooks were feeding in the next field, and he fired!

Such a cackling and screeching as arose! and with it one dying gobble, and a very loud "Hollo! you rascal!"

"My eyes! you've been and gone and done it!" cried Osmond.

"Cut! cut!" screamed Martin; and Hal, not exactly knowing what he had done, but sure that it was something dreadful, and hearing voices in pursuit, threw down the gun, and took to his heels; but the others had the start of him, and were over the gap long before he could get to it. And even as he did reach it, a hand was on his throat, almost choking him, and a tremendous voice cried, "You young poacher, you sha'n't get off that way! I'll have you up to the Bench, that I will, for shooting the poor old turkey-cock before my very eyes."

"Oh! don't, don't! I didn't mean it," cried Hal, turning in the terrible grip; "I thought it was only a rook!"

Charlotte M. Yonge

"A rook, I dare say! And what business had you to think, coming trespassing here on my ground, and breaking the hedges! I'd have you up for that, if for nothing else, you young vagabond!"

"Oh, don't, don't! I'm Henry Merrifield!"

"I don't care if you're Henry Merry Andrew!" said Farmer Grice, who was a surly man, and had a grudge of long standing against the Captain, for withstanding him at the Board of Guardians. "I'll have the law out of you, whoever you are."

"But - but - Mamma is so very ill!" cried Hal, bursting into tears.

"The more shame for you to be rampaging about the country this fashion," said the farmer, giving him a shake that seemed to make all his bones rattle in his skin. "Serve you right if I flogged you within an inch of your life."

"Oh, please don't - I mean please do - anything but have me up to the magistrates! I'll never do it again, never!" sobbed Henry in his terror.

Mr. Grice had some pity, and also knew that his wife and all the neighbours would be shocked at his prosecuting so young a boy, whose parents were in such distress. So he said, "There, then, I'll overlook it this time, sir, so as I have the value of the bird."

"And what is the value - " asked Henry, trembling.

"Value! Why, the breed came from Norfolk; he was three years old; and my missus set great store on him, he was as good as a house-dog, to keep idle children out of the yard; and it was quite a picture to see him posturing about, and setting up his tail! Value! not less than five-and-twenty shillings, sir."

"But I have not five-and-twenty shillings. I can't get them," said Hal, falling back into misery.

"You should have thought of that before you shot poor old Tom Turkey!" quoth Farmer Grice.

"But what in the world shall I ever do?" said Henry.

"That's for you to settle, sir," said the farmer, taking up the unlucky gun. "I shall take this, and keep it out of further harm."

"Oh pray, pray!" cried Henry. "It is not my gun; it is Mr. Greville's; please let me have it!"

"What! was it those young dogs, the Master Grevilles, that were with you!" growled Mr. Grice. "If I'd known that, I'd not have let you off so easy. Those boys are the plague of the place; I wish it had been one of them as I'd caught, I'd have had some satisfaction out of them!"

Henry entreated again for the gun, explaining that they had not leave to take it; but the farmer was unrelenting. He might go to them, he said, to make up the price of the poor turkey-cock; how they could have got the gun was no affair of his; have it they should not, till the money was brought to him; and if it did not come before night, he should carry the gun up to the Park, and complain to Mr. Greville.

With this answer the unhappy Hal was released, and ran after his friends to tell them of the terms. He found them sitting on a low wall, just within their own grounds, waiting to hear what had become of him. When he had told his story, they both set upon him for betraying them, and declared that they should send him to Coventry ever after, and never do anything with him again; but as it was plain that the gun must be redeemed, if they wished to avoid severe punishment, there was a consultation. Nobody had much money; but Osmond consolingly suspected that the farmer would take less; five-and-twenty shillings was an exorbitant price to set on a turkey-cock's head, and perhaps half would content him.

The half, however, seemed as impossible as the whole. Osmond had three shillings, Martin two, Hal four-pence! What was to be done? And the boys declared that if it should come to their father's knowledge, Hal, who had given up their names, should certainly not be shielded by them. In fact, he, who had done the deed, was the only one who ought to pay.

The sound of the servants' dinner-bell at the Park broke up the consultation; the boys must not be missed at luncheon; and they therefore separated, agreeing to meet at that same place at four o'clock, to hear the result of Hal's negotiation with the farmer; for neither of the Grevilles would hear of helping him to face the enemy.

Poor Hal plodded home disconsolately. Once he thought of telling Sam, and asking his help; but Sam would be so much shocked at such a scrape at such a time, as possibly to lick him for it before helping him. Indeed Hal did not see much chance of Sam being able to do anything for them; and he had too often boasted over his elder brother to like to abase himself by such a confession - when, too, it would almost be owning how much better it would have been to have followed Sam's advice and have gone safely to church.

Could he borrow of any one? Had he nothing of his own to sell or exchange? Ah! if it had not been for that stupid hoard of little David's, he might have had even so much! By-the-bye, some of that collection was his own. He might quite lawfully take that back again. How much could it be? How much did he put in last week? The week before? Oh, never mind; some of it was his at all events; there was no harm in taking that. Most likely he should be able to restore it four-fold when Colonel Carey made his present; or, if not, nobody knew exactly what was in Toby Fillpot; and after all very likely they would forget all about it; people could not think about pigs when Mamma was ill; or, maybe, he should go to join his ship, and hear no more of it. So he came home, and crossed the paddock just as the dinner-bell was ringing, opening the hall-door as the children were running across it to the dining-room.

Miss Fosbrook, who was walking behind them, turned as he came in.

"Henry," she said, "I have sent Johnnie to dine in the nursery, for his disobedience in climbing the gate. I certainly shall not give you a less punishment. You must have led him into it; and how could you be so cruel as to leave the poor little fellow alone in such a dangerous place?"

" Stupid little coward! It was not a bit of danger!"

Charlotte M. Yonge

said Hal.

"So young a child - " began Miss Fosbrook.

"Oh, that's all your London notions," said Hal. "Why, I climbed up our gate at Stonehouse, which was twice as high, when I wasn't near as old as that!"

"I am not going to argue with you, Henry; but after such an act of disobedience, I cannot allow you to sit down to dinner with us. Go up to the school-room, and Mary shall bring you your dinner."

"I'm sure I don't want to dine with a lot of babies and governesses!" exclaimed Henry, and bounced up-stairs, leaving Miss Fosbrook quite confounded at such an outbreak of naughtiness.

She intended, as soon as dinner should be over, to go up to him, and try to lead him to be sorry for his conduct, and to think what a wretched moment this was for such audacity; and then she feared that she ought to punish him farther, by keeping him in all the afternoon. He was so soft and easily impressed, that she almost trusted to make him feel that it would be right that he should suffer for his misconduct.

When she went up-stairs, almost as soon as grace had been said, he was gone. Nobody could find him, and calling produced no answer. She became quite distressed and anxious, but could not go far from the house herself, nor send Sam, in case the message should arrive.

"Oh," said Sam, "no doubt he's after something with the Grevilles, and was afraid you would stop him in."

She tried to believe this, but still felt far from satisfied all the afternoon, and was glad to see the boy come back in time for tea.

He said he had been with the Grevilles; he did not see why anybody need ask him questions; he should do what he pleased without being called to account. Nobody told him not to run away after dinner; he was not going to stay to be ordered about for nothing.

This was so bad a temper, that Christabel could not bear to try to touch him with the thought of his sick mother. She knew that softening must come in time, and believed the best thing to do at the moment would be to put a stop to his disrespectful speeches to her, and his cross ones to his brothers and sisters, by sending him to bed as soon as tea was over, as the completion of his punishment. He did not struggle, for she had taught him to mind her; but he went up-stairs with a gloomy brow, and angry murmurs that it was very hard to be put under a stupid woman, who knew nothing about anything, and was always cross.

Charlotte M. Yonge

CHAPTER XII.

Saturday's post brought a letter, and a comfortable one. All Thursday Mrs. Merrifield had been in so doubtful a state, that her husband could not bear to write, lest he should fill the children with false hopes, or alarm them still more; but she had had a good night, was stronger on Friday, and when the post went out, the doctors had just ventured to say they believed she would recover favourably. The letter was finished off in a great hurry; but Captain Merrifield did not forget to thank his little Susan warmly for her poor scrambling letter, and say he knew all she meant by it, bidding her give Miss Fosbrook his hearty thanks for forwarding it, and for telling him the children were all behaving well, and feeling properly. His love to them all; they must try to deserve the great mercy that had been granted to them.

To the children, this was almost as good as saying that their mother was well again; but there was too much awe about them for their joy to show itself noisily. Susan ran away to her own room, and Bessie followed her; and Sam said no word, only Miss Fosbrook remarked that he did not eat two mouthfuls of breakfast. She would not take any notice; she knew his heart was full; and when she looked round on that little flock, and thought of the grievous sorrow scarcely yet averted from them, she could hardly keep the tears from blinding her. They were all somewhat still and grave, and it was too happy a morning to be broken into by the reproofs that Henry deserved, even more richly than Christabel knew. She had almost forgotten his bad behaviour; and when she remembered something of it, she could not but hope that silence, on such a day as this, might bring it home to him more than rebuke. Yet when breakfast was ever, he was among the loudest of those who, shaking off the strange, awed gravity of deep gladness, went rushing together into the garden, feeling that they might give way to their spirits again.

Sam shouted and whooped as if he were casting off a burthen, and picking little George up in his arms, tossed him and swung him round in the air in an ecstasy; while John and Annie and David went down on the grass together, and tumbled and rolled one over the other like three kittens, their legs and arms kicking about, so that it was hard to tell whose property were the black shoes that came wriggling into view.

Susan was quieter. She told Nurse the good news, and then laid hold upon Baby, and carried her off into the passage to hug all to herself. She could tell no one but Baby how very happy she was, and how her heart had trembled at her mother's suffering, her father's grief, and at the desolateness that had so nearly come on them. Oh, she was very happy, very thankful; but she could not scream it out like the others, Baby must have it all in kisses.

"Christabel," said a little voice, when all the others were gone, "I shall never be pipy again."

"You must try to fight against it, my dear."

"Because," said Elizabeth, coming close up to her, "when dear Mamma was so ill, it did seem so silly to mind about not having pretty things like Ida, and the boys plaguing, and so on."

"Yes, my dear; a real trouble makes us ashamed of our little discontents."

"I said so many times yesterday, and the day before, that I would never mind things again, if only Mamma would get well and come home," said the little girl; "and I never shall."

"You will not always find it easy not to mind," said Christabel; "but if you try hard, you will learn how to keep from showing that you mind."

"Oh!" said Elizabeth, (and a great mouthful of an oh! it was,) "those things are grown so silly and little now."

"You have seen them in their true light for once, my dear. And now that you have so great cause of thankfulness to God, you feel that your foolish frets and discontents were unthankful."

"Yes," said Bessie, her eyes cast down, as they always were when anything of this kind was said to her, as if she did not like to meet the look fixed on her.

"Well then, Bessie, try to make the giving up of these murmurs your thank-offering to God. Suppose every day when you say your prayers, you were to add something like this - " and she wrote down on a little bit of paper, "O Thou, who hast raised up my mother from her sickness, teach me to be a thankful and contented child, and to guard my words and thoughts from peevishness."

"Isn't it too small to pray about?" said Elizabeth.

"Nothing is too small to pray about, my dear. Do you think this little midge is too small for God to have made it, and given it life, and spread that mother-of-pearl light on its wings? Do you think yourself too small to pray? or your fault too small to pray about?"

Elizabeth cast down her eyes. She did not quite think it was a fault, but she did not say so.

"Bessie, what was the great sin of the Israelites in the wilderness?"

The colour on her cheek showed that she knew.

"They tempted God by murmurs," said Christabel. "They tried His patience by grumbling, when His care and blessings were all round them, and by crying out because all was not just as they liked. Now, dear Bessie, God has shown you what a real sorrow might be; will it not be tempting Him to go back to complaints over what He has ordained for you?"

"I shall net complain now; I shall not care," said Elizabeth. But she took the little bit of paper, and Christabel trusted that she would make use of it, knowing that in this lay her hope of cure; for whatever she might think in this first joy of relief, her little troubles were sure to seem quite as unbearable while they were upon her as if she had never feared a great one.

However, nothing remarkable happened; everyone was

bright and happy; but still the influence of their past alarm subdued them enough to make them quiet and well-behaved, both on Saturday and Sunday; and Miss Fosbrook had never had so little trouble with them.

In consideration of this, and of the agitation and unsettled state that had put the last week out of all common rules, she announced on Monday morning that she would excuse all the fines, and that all the children should have their allowance unbroken. Maybe she was moved to this by the suspicion that these four sixpences and three threepennies would make up the fund to the price of a "reasonable pig;" and she thought it time that David's perseverance should be rewarded, and room made in his mind for something beyond swine and halfpence.

Her announcement was greeted by the girls with eager thanks, by the boys with a tremendous "Three times three for Miss Fosbrook!" and Bessie was so joyous, that instead of crying out against the noise, she joined in with Susan and Annie; but they made such a ridiculous little squeaking, that Sam laughed at them, and took to mocking their queer thin hurrahs. Yet even this Elizabeth could bear!

David was meanwhile standing by the locker, his fingers at work as if he were playing a tune, his lips counting away, "Ninety-two , ninety-three , ninety-four - that's me; ninety-five, ninety-six, ninety-seven-that's Jack," and so on; till having plodded up diligently, he turned round with a little scream, "One hundred and twenty! That's the pig!"

"What?" cried Annie.

"One hundred and twenty pence. Sukey said one hundred and twenty pence were ten shillings. That will do it! That's the pig! Oh, we've done it! May I take it to Purday?"

"It was to be let alone till fair-day, you little bother!" said Hal.

"No, no, no," cried many voices; "only till we had enough."

"And I am sure nobody knows if we have," added Hal hotly. "A lot of halfpence, indeed!"

"But I know, Hal," insisted David. "There are eighty-nine pence and one farthing in Toby Fillpot, and this makes one hundred and twenty-two pence and one farthing."

"You'd no business to peep," said Sam.

"I didn't peep," said David indignantly. "There were forty-eight pence at first, and then Susie had three, that was fifty-one -" And he would have gone on like a little calculating machine, with the entire reckoning in his head, if the others had had patience to hear; but Annie and Johnnie were urgent to have the sum counted out before their eyes. Hal roughly declared it was against the rules, and little inquisitives must not have their way. But others were also inquisitive; and Sam said it would be best to know how much they had, that Purday might be told to look out for a pig at the price; besides, he wanted to have it over; it was such a bore not to have any money.

" It's not fair!" cried Henry passionately. "You don't

keep the rules! You sha'n't have my sixpence, I can tell you; and I won't - I won't stay and see it."

"Nobody wants you," said Sam.

"I didn't know there were any rules," said the girls; but Hal was already off.

"Hal has only put in fivepence-halfpenny," said David, "so no wonder he is ashamed. Such a big boy, with sixpence a week! But if he won't let us have his sixpence now -"

"Never mind, we will make it up next week," said Susan.

"Now, then, who will take Toby down?" said Miss Fosbrook, unbuttoning one glass door, and undoing the two bolts of the second, behind which the cup of money stood.

"Susie ought, because she is the eldest."

"Davie ought, because he is the youngest."

David stood on a chair to take Toby off his shelf. Solemn was the face with which the little boy lifted the mug by the handle, putting his other hand to steady the expected weight of coppers; but there was at once a frown, a little cry of horror. Toby came up so light in his hand, that all his great effort was thrown away, and only made him stagger back in dismay, falling backward from the chair, and poor Toby crashing to pieces on the floor as he fell, while out rolled - one solitary farthing

Nobody spoke for some moments; but all stood perfectly still, staring as hard as if they hoped the pence would be brought out by force of looking for them.

Then David's knuckles went up into his eyes, and he burst forth in a loud bellow. It was the first time Miss Fosbrook had heard him cry, and she feared that he had been hurt by the fall, or cut by the broken crockery; but he struck out with foot and fist, as if his tears were as much anger as grief, and roared out, "I want the halfpence for my pig."

"Sam, Sam," cried Susan, "if you have hid them for a trick, let him have them."

"I - I play tricks NOW?" exclaimed Sam in indignation. "No, indeed!"

"Then perhaps Hal has," said Elizabeth.

"For shame, Bessie!" cried Sam.

"I only know," said Elizabeth, half in self-defence, half in fright, "that one of you must have been at the baby-house, for I found the doors open, and shut them up."

"And why should it be one of us?" demanded Sam; while David stopped crying, and listened.

"Because none of the younger ones can reach to undo the doors," said Elizabeth. "It was as much as I could do to reach the upper bolt, though I stood upon a chair."

This was evident; for the baby-house was really an

old-fashioned bureau, and below the glass doors there was a projecting slope of polished walnut, upon which only a fly could stand, and which was always locked. No one whose years were less than half a score was tall enough to get a good hold of the button, even from the highest chair, far less to jerk down the rather stiff upper bolt.

"It cannot have been a little one, certainly," said Miss Fosbrook; "but you should not be so ready to accuse your brothers, Bessie."

David, however, had laid hold of a hope, and getting up from the floor, hastened out of the room, followed by John; and they were presently heard shouting "Hal!" all over the house.

"What day was it that you found the door open, Bessie?" asked Miss Fosbrook.

"It was just after dinner," said Elizabeth, recollecting herself.

"It was on Friday. Yes, I remember it was Friday, because I went into the school-room to get my pencil, and I was afraid Hal would jump out upon me, and looked in first to see whether he was going to be tiresome; but he was gone."

"Yes," said Susan; "it was the day we found poor Jack stuck up on the gate, when he and Hal were in disgrace. Oh, he never would have played tricks then."

"Did you go up before me, Bessie?" asked Miss Fosbrook; "for I went up directly after dinner to speak to Henry."

"Yes, I did," said she. "I thought if you got in first, you would be scolding him ever so long, and would let nobody in, so I would get my pencil first; and I slipped up before you had left the table."

Just then the two boys were heard stumping up the stairs, and ran in, panting with haste and excitement, David with a fiery red ear.

"No, no; Hal didn't hide it!"

"But he boxed Davie's ear for thinking he did," added John; "and said he'd do the same for spiteful Bet!"

"Then he never played tricks," said Susan.

"I told you not," said Sam.

"No," reiterated David; "and he said I'd no business to ask; and if Bet went prying about everywhere, I'd better ask her. Have you got it, Betty?"

"I!" cried Elizabeth. "How can you, Davie?"

"You have got a secret," exclaimed David; "and you always were cross about Hannah Higgins's pig. You have got it to tease me! Miss Fosbrook, make her give it back."

"Nonsense, David," said Miss Fosbrook; "Bessie is quite to be trusted; and it is wrong to make unfounded accusations."

"Never mind, Betty," added Sam kindly; "if Davie wasn't a little donkey, he wouldn't say such things."

Charlotte M. Yonge

"Where is Henry?" asked the governess. "Why did he not come himself? Call him; I want to know if he observed this door being open."

"He is gone down to Mr. Carey's," said John.

"And it is high time you were there too, Sam," said Miss Fosbrook, starting. "If you are late, beg Mr. Carey's pardon from me, and tell him that I kept you."

Sam was obliged to run off at full speed; and the other children stood about, still aghast and excited. Miss Fosbrook, however, told them to take out their books. She would not do anything more till she had had time to think, and had composed their minds and her own; for she was exceedingly shocked, and felt herself partly in fault, for having left the hoard in an unlocked cupboard. She feared to do anything hastily, lest she should bring suspicion on the innocent; and she thought all would do better if time were given for settling down. All were disappointed at thus losing the excitement, fancying perhaps that instant search and inquiry would hunt up the money; and David put himself quite into a sullen fit. No, he would not turn round, nor read, nor do anything, unless Miss Fosbrook would make stingy Bet give up the pence.

Miss Fosbrook and Susan both tried to argue with him; but he had set his mind upon one point so vehemently, that it was making him absolutely stupid to everything else; and he was such a little boy (only five years old), that his mind could hardly grasp the exceeding unlikelihood of a girl like Elizabeth committing such a theft, either in sport or earnest, nor understand the injury of such a suspicion. He only knew that she had a secret - a counter secret to his pig; and when she hotly assured him that she had never touched the money, and Susan backed her up with, "There, she says she did not," he answered, "She once told a story."

Elizabeth coloured deep red, and Susan cried out loudly that it was a shame in David; then explained that it was a long long time ago, that Hal and Bessie broke the drawing-room window by playing at ball with little hard apples, and had not 'told, but when questioned had said, "No;" but indeed they had been so sorry then that she knew they would never do so again.

Again David showed that he could not enter into this, and sulkily repeated, "She told a story."

"I will have no more of this," said Christabel resolutely. "You are all working yourselves up into a bad spirit: and not another word will I hear on this matter till lessons are over."

That tone was always obeyed; but lessons did not prosper; the children were all restless and unsettled; and David, hitherto for his age her best scholar, took no pains, and seemed absolutely stupefied. What did he care for fines, if the chance of the pig was gone? And he was sullenly angry with Miss Fosbrook for using no measures to recover the money, fancied she did not care, and remembered the foolish nursery talk about her favouring Bessie.

Once Miss Fosbrook heard a little gasping from the corner, and looking round, saw poor Bessie crying quietly over her slate, and trying hard to check herself. She would not have noticed her, though longing to comfort her, if David had not cried out, "Bet is crying! A fine!"

"No," said Miss Fosbrook; "but a fine for an ill-natured speech that has made her cry."

"She has got the pig's money," muttered David.

"Say that again, and I shall punish you, David."

He looked her full in the face, and said it again.

She was thoroughly roused to anger, and kept her word by opening the door of a small dark closet, and putting David in till dinner-time.

Then she and Susan both tried to soothe Bessie, by reminding her how childish David was, how he had caught up some word that probably Hal had flung out without meaning it, and how no one of any sense suspected her for a moment.

"It is so ill-natured and hard," sobbed Bessie. "To think I could steal! I think they hate me."

"Ah," said Susan, "if you only would never be cross to the boys, Bessie, and not keep out of what they care for, they would never think it."

"Yes, Susie is right there," said Christabel. "If you try to be one with the others, and make common cause with them, giving up and forbearing, they never will take such things into their heads."

"And WE don't now," said Susan cheerily. "Didn't you hear Sam say nobody but a donkey could think it?"

"But Bessie has a secret!" said Annie.

Again stout Susan said, "For shame!"

"I'll tell you what my secret is," began Bessie.

"No," said Susan, "don't tell it, dear! We'll trust you without; and Sam will say the same."

Bessie flung her arms round Susan's neck, as if she only now knew the comfort of her dear good sister.

Lessons were resumed; and as soon as these were done, Miss Fosbrook resolved on a thorough search. Some strange fit of mischief or curiosity might have actuated some one, and the money be hidden away; so she brought David out of his cupboard, and with Susan's help turned out every drawer and locker in the school-room, forbidding the others to touch or assist. They routed out queer nests of broken curiosities, disturbed old dusty dens of rubbish, peeped behind every row of books; but made no discovery worth mentioning, except the left leg of Annie's last doll, the stuffing of Johnnie's ball, the tiger out of George's Noah's ark, and the first sheet of Sam's Latin Grammar, all stuffed together into a mouse-hole in the skirting.

At dinner Christabel forbade the subject to be mentioned, not only to hinder quarrelsome speeches, but to prevent the loss being talked of among the servants; since she feared that one of them must have committed the theft, and though anxious not to put it into the children's heads, suspected Rhoda, the little nursery-girl, who was quite a child, and had not long been in the house.

Henry ate his dinner in haste, but could not get away

Charlotte M. Yonge

till Miss Fosbrook had called him away from the rest, and told him that if he had been playing a trick on his little brother, it was time to put an end to it, before any innocent person fell under suspicion.

"I - I've been playing no tricks - at least -"

"Without any AT LEAST, Henry, have you hidden the money?"

"No."

"You dined in the school-room on Friday. Were the baby-house doors open then!"

"I - I'm sure I didn't notice."

"You didn't open them to take anything out?"

"What should I want with the things in the baby-house?"

"Did you, or did you not!"

"I - I didn't - at least -"

"In one word, did you open them? yes or no."

"No."

"What time did you go out after eating your dinner?"

"Bother! how is one to remember! It's all nonsense making such a fuss. The children fancied they put in ever so much more than they did, and very likely took out some."

"No; David's reckoning was accurate. I wrote down all I knew of; and I am sure none was taken out, for early that very morning I had put in a sixpence myself, and the cup was then full of coppers, with that little silver threepenny of David's with the edge turned up upon the top."

"Then you must have left the door undone!" said Henry delighted.

"I dare not be positive," said Christabel; "but I believe I remember bolting it; and if I had not done so, it would have flown open sooner."

"Oh, but the wind, you know."

"If the doors did open, it would not account for the loss of the money."

"Well, I can't help it," said Henry ungraciously, trying to move off: but she first required him to tell her what he had said to the younger boys to make them suspect Elizabeth.

"Did I?" said Henry, "I am sure I didn't; at least, if I did, I only said Bess peeped everywhere, and was very close. I didn't suspect her, you know."

"I should think not!" said Miss Fosbrook indignantly. "Now please to come up with me."

"I want to go out," said Henry.

No, she would not let him go. She thought Elizabeth ought to clear herself, so far as it could be done, by making her secret known, since that had drawn suspicion on her; and when all the children were together, she called the little girl and told her so.

"It is very unkind of them," said Bessie, with trembling lip; "but they shall see, if they want THAT to show I am not a thief!"

"I said I wouldn't see," said Susan. "You knows Bessie, I trust you."

"And I," said Sam; "I don't care for people's secrets. I don't want to pry into Bessie's."

No one followed their example; all either really suspected, or else were full of curiosity, and delighted to gratify it.

Half a dozen slips of card, with poor little coloured drawings on them, and as many lengths of penny ribbon!

"Is that all?" said Annie, much disappointed.

"So that's what Bet made such a fuss about," said John; and David's face fell, as if he had really expected to see the lost pence.

The next thing, after the search had been made through all the children's bed-rooms, was to go to the nursery: and thither Miss Fosbrook allowed only Susan and Sam to follow her. Nurse Freeman was very stiff and stately, but she had no objection to searching; and the boy and girl began the hunt, while Miss Fosbrook meantime cautiously asked whether Nurse were sure of Rhoda, and if she were trustworthy.

This made Mrs. Freeman very angry; and though her words were respectful, she showed that she was much offended at the strange lady presuming to suspect anyone, especially one under her charge.

Miss Fosbrook wanted to have asked Rhoda whether the doors were open or shut when she carried Henry his dinner, but Nurse would not consent to call her. "I understood the nursery and the girl were to be my province," she said. "If Miss Merrifield heard her mamma say otherwise, then it is a different thing."

Susan cowered into the dark cupboard. Nurse must be in a dreadful way to call her Miss Merrifield, instead of Missy!

Nothing more could be done. The pence could not be found. Nurse would not let Rhoda be examined; and all that could be found out from the children had been already elicited.

Christabel could only beg that no more should be said, and, her head aching with perplexity, hope that some light might yet be thrown on the matter. There must be pain and grief whenever it should be explained; but this would be far better, even for the offender, than the present deception: and the whole family were in a state of irritation and distrust, that hurt their tempers, and made her bitterly reproach herself with not having prevented temptation by putting the hoard under lock and key.

She ordered that no more should be said about it that evening, and made herself obeyed; but play was dull, and everything went off heavily. The next morning, Susan came back early from her housekeeping business, with her honest face grave and unhappy, and finding Miss Fosbrook alone, told her she had something REALLY to say to her if she might; and this being granted began, with the bright look of having found a capital notion: "I'll tell you what I wish you would do."

"Well?"

"If you would call every one in all the house, and ask them on their word and honour if they took the pence."

"My dear, I am not the head of the house, and I have no right to do that; besides, I do not believe it would discover it."

"What! could a thief get in from out of doors!" said Susan looking at the window.

"Hardly that, my dear; but I am afraid a person who could steal would not scruple to tell a falsehood, and I do not wish to cause this additional sin."

"It is very horrid; I can't bear it," said Susan, puckering up her face for tears. "Do you know, Miss Fosbrook, the maids are all so angry that you said anything about Rhoda?"

"You did not mention it, my dear?"

"Oh no; nor Sam. It was Nurse herself! But they all say that you want to take away her character; and they won't have strangers put over them."

"Pray, Susie; don't tell me this. It can do no good."

"Oh, but PLEASE!" cried Susan. "And then Mary - I can't think how she could - but she said that poor dear Bessie was always sly, and that she had been at the cupboard, and had got the pence; but she was your favourite, and so you vindicated her. And Nurse began teasing her to confess, and tell the truth, and told her she was a wicked child because she would not; but it was all because we were put under strangers! I'm sure they do set on Johnnie and Davie to be cross to her."

"When was this, my dear?"

"Last night, when we went to the nursery to be washed. It was our night, you know. Oh! I wish Mamma was well!"

"Indeed I do my dear. And how did poor Bessie bear it!"

"She got quite white, and never said a word, even when they told her she was sulky. But when we got into bed, and I kissed her and cuddled her up, oh! she did cry so; I didn't know what to do. So, do you know, I got my shawl on, and went and called Sam; and he was not gone to sleep, and he came and sat by her, and told her that he believed her, and knew she was as sound a heart of oak as any of us; and we both petted her, and Sam was so nice and kind, till she went to sleep. Then he went to the nursery, and told Nurse how horrid it was in her; but Cook said it only made her worse, because she is jealous of our taking part with you."

"My dear, I DO like to hear of your kindness to Bessie; but I wish you would not mind what any of the maids say , nor talk to them about it. It only distresses you for nothing."

"But I can't help it," said Susan.

"You could not help this attack in the nursery, but you need not talk to Cook or Mary about it. It is of no use to vex ourselves with what people say who don't know half a story."

"Can't you tell them not?" said simple Susan.

"No, I cannot interfere. They would only do it the more. We can only keep Bessie as much out of the way of the maids as we can, and show our confidence in her."

Certainly Elizabeth had been known to look infinitely more glum when nothing was the matter than under all this vexation, even though the servants were really very unkind to her; and her two little brothers both behaved as ill as possible to her whenever they had the opportunity - David really believing that she had made away with the money, and ought to be tortured for it; and Johnnie taking it on his word, and being one of those little boys who have a positive taste for ill-nature, and think it fun. They pinched her, they bit her, they rubbed out her sums, they shut up her lesson-books and lost her place, they put bitten crusts into her plate, and did whatever they knew she most disliked, whenever Miss Fosbrook or Sam was not in the way; but she never told. She did not choose to be called a tell-tale; and besides, they really did not succeed in making her life miserable, so much was she pleased with the real kindness her trouble had brought out from Susan and Sam. Susan could not prevent the persecution of the two naughty little boys, but she defended her sister to her utmost; and Sam cuffed them if they said a word or lifted a finger against Bessie before him; and he gave her such notice and kindness as she never had received from him before. One afternoon, when he was going to walk to Bonchamp, he asked leave for her to come with him, and would take nobody else; and hot day as it was, Bessie had never had such a charming walk. She kept herself from making one single fuss; and in return, he gathered wild strawberries for her, showed her a kingfisher, and took her to look in at a very grand aquarium in the fishing-tackle maker's window, where she saw some gold-fish, and a most comical little newt. And going home, they had a real good talk about their father's voyage, and how they should get on without him; and Bessie found to her great pleasure, that Sam hoped Miss Fosbrook would stay when Mamma Came home.

"For I do think she has put some sense into you, Bessie," said Sam.

She was so delighted, that instead of preparing to fret if Sam did but hold up a finger at her, she looked up with a smile when he came in her way, sure of protection, and expecting something pleasant, as well as thinking it an honour to be asked to help him in anything. The next day, when Mr. Carey had insisted on his verifying by the map all the towns which he had been contented to say were in Asia Minor (where every place in ancient history is always put if its whereabouts be doubtful), she saved him so much time and trouble, that he got out into the garden full half an hour earlier than he would otherwise have done. Thereupon he told her she was a jolly good fellow, and gave her such a thump on the back, as a few weeks ago would have made her scream and whine; but this time she took it as

Charlotte M. Yonge

a new form of thanks, and felt highly honoured by being invited to help him to fish for minnows, though it almost made her sick to stick the raw meat upon his hooks.

The threatening of a true sorrow, the bearing a real trouble, and the opening to her brother's kindness, had done far more to make her a happy little girl than all Miss Fosbrook's attempts to satisfy her cravings or please her tastes. These had indeed done her some good, and taught her to find means of enjoyment for those likings that no one else cared for; but it had been the SPIRIT of delight that had been chiefly wanting; and when thankfulness and love were leading her to that, it was much easier to see that the evening clouds or the rising moon were lovely, than when she was looking out for affronts.

Nothing was said in public about the loss; and Christabel hoped that the bad impression as to Elizabeth would wear out in the young minds of the lesser children; but David's whole nature seemed to have been disorganized by the disappointment. Instead of being a pattern child for diligence and good behaviour, very fond of Miss Fosbrook, and not only inoffensive, but often keeping John and Anne in order, he seemed absolutely stupid and senseless at lessons, became stubborn at reproof, seemed to take pleasure in running counter to his governess, and rendered the other two, who, though his elders, were both of weak natures compared with his own, more openly naughty than himself. Sometimes it seemed to Christabel that the habit of spiting Bessie was getting so confirmed, that it would last even when the cause was forgotten; and yet the more she strove to put it down in sight, the more it throve out of sight; and when she looked at

David, and thought how she had once admired him, she could not but remember the text that says, "Thy goodness is as the morning cloud, and as the dew shall it vanish away." She had thought it goodness based upon religious feeling, as well as on natural gravity and orderliness; and so perhaps it had once been, but the little fellow had fixed his whole soul on one purpose, and though that was a good one, it had grown into an idol, and swallowed up all his other motives, till of late he had only been good for the sake of the pig, not because it was right. Being disappointed of the pig, he had nothing to fall back upon, but felt himself so ill-used, that it seemed to him that it was no use to be good; and he revenged himself by naughtiness.

Such sturdy strong characters as little David's, when they are once set on the right object, come to the very best kind of goodness; but when they take a wrong turn, they are the very worst, both for themselves and others.

CHAPTER XIII.

The Monday after the loss of the pence was a pouring wet day. The whole court was like a flood, and the drops went splashing up again as if in play; Purday wore his master's old southwester coat, and looked shiny all over; and when the maids had to cross the court, they went click, click, in their pattens under their umbrellas.

But it was baking day, and Susan and Annie had been down to coax the cook into making them a present of a handsome allowance of dough, and Miss Fosbrook into letting them manipulate it in the school-room. Probably this was the only way of preventing the dough from being turned into bullets, and sent flying at each other's eyes, or possibly plastered on somebody's nose, and the cook and kitchenmaid from being nearly driven crazy.

The dough was justly divided, and an establishment set up in each locker. Bessie declined altogether; Sam had lent her his beautiful book of The British Songsters, and she was hard at work at the table copying a tom-tit, since she no longer carried on the work in secret; but at one locker were the other three elders, at the other the three lesser ones, and little George in a corner by Susan, pegging away at his own private lump, and constantly begging for more. Susan's ambition was to make a set of real twists, just like Cook's; and she pulled out and twisted and plaited, though often robbed of her dough by the two boys, whose united efforts were endeavouring to produce a likeness of Purday, with his hat on his head, plums for eyes, a pipe in his mouth, and driving a cow; but unluckily his neck always got pinched off, and his arms would not stay on! No matter; the more moulding of that soft dough the better! Johnnie and Annie had a whole party of white clammy serpents, always being set to bite one another, and to melt into each other; and David was hard at work on a brood of rabbits with currant eyes, and would let no one interfere with him.

"Didn't I hear something!" asked Bessie, looking up.

"Oh, it's only the roller," said Sam; "Purday always rolls on a wet day."

Something, however, made the whole party of little bakers hold up their heads to listen. There was a gleam on their faces, as a quick alert step sounded on the stairs, and Bessie, the nearest to the door, and not cramped like the rest, who were sitting on their heels, sprang forward and opened it with a scream of joy.

There he was - the light, alert, weather-beaten man, with his loose wavy hair, and bright sailor face! There was Papa! Oh, the hurly-burly of children, tumbling up as well as they could on legs crooked under them, and holding out great fans of floury doughy paws, all coming to be hugged in his arms in turn, so that before he had come to the end of the eight in presence, Bessie had had time to whisk off to the nursery, snatch Baby up from before Nurse's astonished eyes, rush down with her, and put her into his arms. Baby had forgotten him, and was taken with such a fit of screaming shyness, that Susan had to take her, and Annie to play bo-peep with her, before she would let anyone's voice be heard.

"I've taken you by surprise, Miss Fosbrook," said the Captain, shaking hands with her in the midst of the clatter.

"Oh, it is such a pleasure!" she began. "I hope you left Mrs. Merrifield much better."

"Much better, much better, thank you. I hope to find her on the sofa when I go back on Thursday. I could only run down for a few days, just to settle things, and see the children, before I join the Ramilies. Admiral Penrose very good-naturedly kept it open for me, till we could tell how SHE was," said the Captain, with rather a trembling voice.

"Then you are going! O Papa!" said Susan, looking up at him; "and Baby will not know you till -"

"Hold your tongue, Miss Croaker," said the Captain, roughly but kindly; and Miss Fosbrook could see that he was as much afraid of crying himself as of letting Susan cry; "I've no time for that. I've got a gentleman on business down stairs, and your Uncle John and I must go down to them again. We sha'n't want dinner; only, Sue, tell them to send in some eggs and bacon, or cold meat, or whatever there may be, for tea; and get a room ready for your uncle."

He would have gone, but Susan called out, "O Papa, may we drink tea with you, Georgy and all!"

"Yes, to be sure, if you won't make a bear-fight, any of you, for your uncle."

"Mayn't I come down with you?" added Sam, looking at him as if he wanted to make the most of every moment of that presence.

"Better not, my boy," said the Captain; "I've got law business to settle, and we don't want you. Better stay and make yourselves decent for tea-time. Mamma's love, and she hopes you'll not drive Uncle John distracted." And he was gone.

"Bother Uncle John!" first muttered Sam (I am sorry to say).

"I can't think what he's come for," sighed Annie.

"To spoil our fun," suggested Johnnie disconsolately.

"To take Sam to school," added Hal, "while I go to sea."

"You don't know that you are going," said Elizabeth. "Papa said nothing about it."

"Oh! but I know I shall. Admiral Penrose promised."

"You know a great many things that don't happen. You knew Colonel Carey would give you two sovereigns."

Henry looked as if he could bite.

"Well, I shall finish Purday," said Sam, turning away with a sigh; "and they shall have him for tea."

Charlotte M. Yonge

"Tea will be no fun!" repeated Annie. "Oh dear! what does Uncle John come here for?"

"May not he come to be with his brother?" suggested Christabel.

"Oh! but they are grown up," said Annie.

"Can't he have him in London, without coming here to worry us in our little time!" added Johnnie.

"Perhaps he will not worry you."

"Oh! but - " they all cried, and stopped short.

"He plagues about manners," said Annie.

"He wanted Susie and me to be sent to school!" said Bessie.

"He said it was like dining with young Hottentots."

"He told Papa it was disgraceful, when we had all been sliding on the great pond in the village," added Annie.

"And he gave Sam a box on the ear, for only just taking a dear little river cray-fish in his fishing-net to show Aunt Alice."

"The net was dripping wet," observed Bessie.

"Yes," said Anne; "but Aunt Alice is so finikin and fidgety; she never wets her feet, and can't get over a stile, and is afraid of a cow; and he wants us all to be like her."

"And he makes Papa and Mamma mind things that they don't mind by nature," said Susan.

"Mamma always tells us to be good, and never play at hockey in the house when he's there," said Anne.

"She has not told us so this time," said John triumphantly.

"No, but we must mind all the same," said Susan; and Sam silenced some independent murmurs, about not minding Uncle John, by saying it was minding Mamma.

Miss Fosbrook herself was a little alarmed, for she gathered that Mamma was in some fear of this terrible uncle, that he had much influence with his brother, and was rather a severe judge of the young family. She sincerely hoped that he would not find things much amiss, for the honest goodness of the two eldest had won so much regard from her, that she could not bear them to be under any cloud; and indeed she felt as if the whole flock were her own property, as well as her charge, and that she, as well as they, were about to be tried. She would have felt it all fair and just before their kindly father, but it seemed hard that all should be brought before the school-master uncle; and she was disposed to be tender for her children, and exceedingly anxious as to the effect they might produce. She was resolved that the Captain should hear of the affair of the pence; but the presence of his brother would make the speaking a much greater effort. Meantime, she saw that all the fingers were clean, and all the hair brushed. She flattered herself that Susan's yellow locks had learnt that it was the business of hair to keep tidy, and had been much less unmanageable of late; but she had

Charlotte M. Yonge

her fears that they would ruffle up again when their owner, at the head of a large detachment, rushed out to take the "fancy bread" out of the oven, and she came half-way down stairs, in case it should be necessary to capture them, and brush them over again.

While thus watching, the door of the dining-room (the only down stairs room in order) opened suddenly, and the Captain came forth. "Oh, Miss Fosbrook," he said, "please come in here: I was just coming to look for you. My brother - Miss Fosbrook."

To her surprise, Miss Fosbrook received a very pleasant civil greeting from a much younger man than she had expected to see, looking perhaps more stern about the mouth and sharp about the eye than his elder brother, and his clerical dress very precise; but somehow he was so curiously like his niece, Elizabeth, that she thought that his particularity might spring from the same love of refinement.

"All going on well?" asked the Captain.

"Fairly well," she answered. "Sam and Susan are most excellent children. There is only one matter on which I should like to speak to you, at some time when it might suit you."

"Is it about this?" he said, putting into her hand a sheet written in huge round-hand in pencil, no words misspelt, but the breaks in them at the end of the lines perfectly regardless of syllables:-

My dear Papa,

Please let me

have a poli
ceman. Bet h
as got at Toby
and stole our
pence which was
for a secret. Nu
rse says she is a
favourite and Miss
Fosbrook will not
find them.

Your affectionate son

DAVID DOUGLAS MERRIFIELD.

"Oh! this was the letter David insisted on sealing before I put it into mine!" exclaimed Miss Fosbrook, as soon as she had made out the words. "We have been in great trouble at the loss; but we agreed not to write to you, because you had so much on your mind."

"Is Bessie in fault?"

"No, no; none of us believe it; but I am very anxious that you should make an investigation, for the maids suspect her, and have made the younger children do so."

"And who is Toby?"

"Toby is only a jug - called Toby Fillpot, I believe - shaped like a man."

"I know!" put in Mr. John Merrifield, laughing. "Don't you remember him, Harry ? We had the like in

Charlotte M. Yonge

our time."

"Well?" interrogated the Captain.

"Just after you left home," said Christabel, as shortly and clearly as she could, "the children agreed to save their allowance to buy a pig for Hannah Higgins. They showed great perseverance in their object; and by the third week they had about seven shillings in this jug, which, to my grief and shame, I let them keep in the glass cupboard, not locked, but one door bolted, the other buttoned. On Friday morning, the 11th, I know the cup was full of coppers and silver, for I took it down to add something to it. On the next Monday morning the money was gone, all but one farthing."

"Can you guess who took it?"

"I should prefer saying nothing till you have examined the children and servants for yourself."

"Right!" said the Captain. "Very well. - I am sorry to treat you to a court-martial, John, but I must hold one after tea."

Christabel pitied the children for having to speak before this formidable uncle; but there could be no help for it, since no other sitting-room was habitable, and there were torrents of rain out-of-doors.

There was just time to show the glass cupboard, and the shelf where Toby had stood, and to return to the dining-room, before the children began to stream in and make their greetings to their uncle, Susan with George in one hand, and her plate of bakings in the other. Very fancy bread indeed it was! as Uncle John said. The edge of Purday's hat had been quite baked off, and one of his arms was gone; he was black in the wrong places, and was altogether rather an uncomfortable-looking object. David's brood of rabbits were much more successful, though the ears of many had fallen off. Uncle John was very much diverted, and took his full share of admiring and tasting the various performances. On the whole, the meal went off much better than Christabel had feared it would. She had really broken the children of many of the habits with which they used to make themselves disagreeable; there was no putting of spoons into each other's cups, nor reaching out with buttery fingers; lips were wiped, and people sat still upon their chairs, even if they fidgeted and sighed; and there was only one slop made all tea-time, and that was by Johnnie, and not a very bad one. Indeed, it might be hoped that Mr. Merrifield did not see it, for he was talking to Sam about the change of footpath that Mr. Greville was making. There was indeed no fun, but it might be doubted whether Papa would have been in a mood for fun even had his brother not been there; and Miss Fosbrook was rather glad there was nothing to make the children forgetful of propriety.

As soon as Mary had carried off the tea-things and wiped the table, Uncle John put himself as much out of the way as he could behind the newspaper in the recess of the window; and Miss Fosbrook would have gone to the school-room, but Captain Merrifield begged her to stay.

"I hear," he said, "that a very unpleasant thing has taken place in my absence, and I wish to learn all that I can about it, that the guilty person may be brought to light, and the innocent cleared from any suspicion."

The children looked at one another, wondering how he had heard, or whether Miss Fosbrook had told him; but this was soon answered by his calling out, "David! come here, and tell me what you meant by this letter."

David walked stoutly to his father's knee, nothing daunted, though his brothers muttered behind him, "So he wrote!" "Little sneak!" and "He knew no better!" Not that it was wrong to lay the case before his father; but boys had usually rather suffer injustice than make an accusation.

"Why did you write this letter, David?" said his father.

"Because I want my pence for the pig."

"Tell me how you lost them?"

"Bess took them!"

Elizabeth sprung up, crimson, and with tears in her eyes, and Sam and Susan were both bursting out into an angry "No, no!" but their father made a sign to all to keep still; and they obeyed, though each of the elder ones took hold of a hand of their sister and squeezed it hard.

"Did you see her take them?" asked the Captain.

"No!"

"Then why do you say she did? I don't want to frighten you, David; I only want to hear why you think she did so."

David was getting alarmed now , and his childish

memory better retained the impression than what had produced it. He hung down his head, scraped one foot, and finding that he must answer, mumbled out at last, "Nurse said it, and Hal."

"Henry, come here. Did you accuse your sister to David?"

"No!" burst out Henry at once; but there was a rounding of everyone's mouth to cry out Oh! and he quickly added, in a hasty scared way, "At least, when Davie came bothering me, I said he had better ask Betty, because she had been prying about, and meddling with the baby-house. I never meant that she had done it; but Davie is such a little jack-ass!"

"Did you see her meddle with the baby-house!"

"She said that herself," muttered Henry.

"Yes, Papa," said Elizabeth, starting forward, "I did find the doors of the baby-house open, and shut them up, but I never touched anything in it! Sam and Susie know I would not, and that I would not tell a story now, though I once did, you know, Papa!"

Captain Merrifield still kept his grave set face, and only asked, "When did you find the doors open?"

"On Friday, Papa - Friday week - St. Barnabas' Day - just after dinner."

"Was no one with you?"

"No, Papa."

Charlotte M. Yonge

"You came up-stairs first?"

"Yes; I wanted my pencil before - " and she stopped short.

"Before what?"

"Before Miss Fosbrook went in to speak to Hal," said Elizabeth, getting red all over.

"Hal had been dining in the school-room," said Miss Fosbrook, "on account of a little bit of disobedience."

Captain Merrifield looked keenly at Henry, who tried to return the look, but shuffled uncomfortably under it.

"Then Hal had been dining in the school-room? Was he there when you came in?"

"No."

"Were the doors open when you were dining there, Henry?"

"N - no."

"You are sure that you did not meddle with them?"

"I do not know why I should," said Henry, hastily and confusedly. "It is only the girls and the babies that have things there - and - and Miss Fosbrook herself had been at the cupboard in the morning; why shouldn't she have left it undone herself, and the doors got open?"

" No, no!" cried Susan; "if they aren't fastened they

always burst open directly; and we never could have been in the room half the morning without noticing them!"

"Then you are certain that they were closed when you went down to dinner?"

Everyone was positive that the great glass doors flying out must have made themselves observed in that room full of children, especially as Susan remembered that she had been making a desk of the sloping part under them.

"Does anyone remember how long it was between Hal's leaving the room and Bessie's coming up?"

"I don't know when he went out," said all those who had been in the dining-room; but there spoke up a voice, quite proud of having something to tell among the others - "I saw Hal go out, and Bessie come up directly."

"You, Johnnie! How was that?"

"Miss Fosbrook made me dine in the nursery, Papa, because Hal and I had been riding on the new iron gate, to see if the telegraph would come in while the others were at church; and then Hal ran away with the Grevilles, and I couldn't get down till Sam came and helped me; and so Miss Fosbrook made me dine in the nursery; and when I had done, I went and sat upon the top of the garret stairs, to watch when they came out from dinner, and ask if I might come down again."

"And what did you see, Johnnie?"

"First, I saw a wasp," said Johnnie.

"Never mind the wasp. Did you see when Henry went out?"

"I saw him come in first," said John, "and Miss Fosbrook order him up and say she would send him his dinner, and come and speak to him presently. So I watched to catch her when she was coming up to him, and I saw Mary bring him up some mince veal, and the last bit of the gooseberry pie; and then, very soon, he bolted right downstairs. I didn't think he could have had time to eat the pie; and I was going to see if there was a bit left, when I saw Bessie coming up, and I whipped up again."

"Then nobody went into the room between Henry and Bessie?"

"No; there wasn't any time."

The whole room was quite silent. There was no sound but a quick short breathing from the Captain: but he had rested his brow upon his hand, and his face could not be seen. It was as if something terrible had flashed upon him, and he was struggling with the first shock, and striving to deal with it. If they had seen him in a tempest, with his ship driving to pieces on a rock, he would not have been thus shaken and dismayed. However, by the time he looked up again, he had brought his face back to its resolute firmness, and he spoke in a clear, stern, startling voice, that made all the children quake, and some catch hold of each other's hands: "Henry! tell me what you have done with your theft!"

Miserable Henry! He did not try to deny it any longer; but burst out into a loud sobbing cry, "O Papa! Papa! I meant to have put it back again! I couldn't help it!"

"Tell me what you have done with it!" repeated the Captain.

"I - I paid it to Farmer Grice; I was obliged; and I thought I could have put it back again; and some of it was my own!"

"Fivepence-farthing!" cried David. "You thief, you!"

The child's fists were clenched, and his young face all one scowl of passion, quite shocking to see. His father put him aside, and said, "Hush, David! no names. - Now, Henry, what do you say to your sister for your false accusation, which has thrown your own shame on her?"

"Oh, no, no, Papa; he never did accuse me!" cried Bessie, for the first time bursting into tears. "He never said I did it; that was only Davie's fancy; and it has made Susie and Sam so kind, I have not minded it at all. Please don't mind that, Papa!"

"Come away, Henry!" said the Captain; "now that your sister has been cleared, we had better have the rest out of the sight of these tender-hearted little girls."

He stood up, and without a word, stroked down Elizabeth's smooth brown hair, raised her face up by the chin, and kissed her forehead, the only place free from tears; then he took Henry by the shoulder, and marched him out of the room. Bessie could not stop herself from crying, and was afraid of letting Uncle

John see her; so she flew out after them, and straight up-stairs to her own room. Miss Fosbrook and Susan both longed to follow her, but they had missed this opportunity; and the sound of voices outside showed so plainly that the Captain and Henry were in the hall that they durst not open the door.

Everyone was appalled, and nothing was said for a few seconds. The first to speak was Annie, in a low, terror-stricken whisper, yet with some curiosity in it: "I wonder what Papa will do to him?"

"Give him nine dozen, I hope!" answered David through his small white teeth, all clenched together with rage.

"For shame, Davie!" said Susan; "you should not wish anything so dreadful for your brother."

"He has been so wicked! I wish it! I WILL wish it!" said David.

"Hush, David!" said Miss Fosbrook; "such things must not be said. I will talk to you by and by."

"I am glad poor Bessie is cleared!" added Susan; "though I always knew she could not have done it."

"To be sure - I knew it was Hal!"

"Sam! you did? - why didn't you tell?" cried Annie.

"I wasn't - to say - sure," said Sam; "and I couldn't go and get him into a scrape. I thought he might tell himself, if he could ever make up the money again!"

"Yes," said Susan; "he would have done that. He always fancied he should get a sovereign from Colonel Carey."

"He talked till he thought so," said Sam.

"But what made you guess he had done so, Sam?" said Miss Fosbrook. "I did suspect him myself, but I never felt justified in accusing him of such a thing."

"I don't know! I saw he had been getting into a fix with those Grevilles, and had been sold somehow. They said something, and got out of my way directly, and I was sure they had done some mischief, and left him to pay the cost."

"Did you ask him?" said Susan.

"What was the use? One never knows where to have him. He will eat up his words as fast as he says them, with his AT LEAST, till he doesn't know what he means. Nor I didn't want to know much of it."

"Still I can't think how you could let poor Bessie live under such a cloud," said Christabel.

"You didn't believe it," said Sam, "nor anyone worth a snap of my finger. Besides, if I had known, and had to tell, what a horrid shame it would have been if the naval cadetship had been to be had for him! I knew Bessie would have thought so too, and then he would have been out of the way of the Grevilles, and would have got some money to make it up."

"Then is there no chance of the cadetship now?"

Charlotte M. Yonge

"Oh, we should have heard of it long ago if there had been! So I mind the coming out the less; but it's perfectly abominable to have had all this row, and for Papa to be so cut up in this little short time at home."

"I never saw him more grieved," said Mr. Merrifield. "He was hardly more overcome when your mother was at the worst."

They started, for they had forgotten Uncle John, or they would never have spoken so freely; but he now put down his newspaper, and looked as if he meant to talk.

Susan ventured to say, "And indeed they had all been so very good before. The pig made them so."

"A learned pig, I should think," said her uncle, laughing good-naturedly.

"We were obliged to take care," said Susan, "or we got so many fines."

Christabel, finding that Mr. Merrifield looked at her, helped out Susan by explaining that various small delinquencies were visited with fines, and that the desire to save for the pig had rendered the children very careful.

"Indeed," she said, "I was thankful for the incentive, but I am afraid that it was over-worked, and did harm in the end:" and she glanced towards David.

"It is the way with secondary motives," was the answer.

Here Captain Merrifield came back alone; and his brother was the only person who ventured to say, "Well?"

"I have sent him to his room," said the Captain. "It is a very bad business, though of course he made excuses to himself."

The Captain then told them Henry's confession. He had been too much hurried by the fear of being caught, to take out his own share of the hoard, and had therefore emptied the whole cupful into his pocket-handkerchief, tied it up, and run off with it, intending to separate what was honestly his own. What that was he did not know, but his boastful habits and want of accuracy had made his memory so careless, that he fancied that a far larger proportion was his than really was, and his purposes were in the strange medley that falls to the lot of all self-deceivers, sometimes fancying he would only take what he had a right to (whatever that might be), sometimes that he would borrow what he wanted, and replace it when the sovereign should be given to him, or that the Grevilles would make it up when they had their month's allowance.

When he came to the farm Mr. Grice was resolved to take nothing less than the whole sum that he had with him. Perhaps this was less for the value of the turkey-cock than for the sake of giving the boys such a lesson as to prevent them from ever molesting his poultry again. At any rate, he was inexorable till the frightened Henry had delivered up every farthing in his possession; and then, convinced that no more was forthcoming, he relented so far as to restore the gun, and promise to make no complaint to either of the fathers.

Charlotte M. Yonge

At first Henry lived on hopes of being able to restore the money before the hoard should be examined, but Colonel Carey went away, and, as might have been expected, left no present to his brother's pupils. Still Henry had hopes of the Grevilles, and even when the loss was discovered, hoped to restore it secretly, and make the whole pass off as a joke; but the 1st of August came, Martin and Osmond received their pocket-money, but laughed his entreaty to scorn, telling him that he had shot the turkey-cock, not they. Since that time, his only hope had been in the affair blowing over - as if a sin ever DID blow over!

"One question I must ask, Miss Fosbrook," said the Captain, "though after such a course of deceit it hardly makes it worse. Has he told any direct falsehood?"

She paused, and recollected. "Yes, Sir," she said, "I am afraid he did; he flatly told me that he had not touched the baby-house."

"I expected nothing else," said the Captain gravely. "What has become of Bessie?"

"She ran up-stairs. May I go and call her?" said Susan.

"I will go myself," said her father.

He found Elizabeth in the school-room, all flushed and tear-stained in the face; and he told her affectionately how much pleased he was with her patience under this false accusation. Delight very nearly set her off crying again, but she managed to say, "It was Miss Fosbrook and Sam and Susie that made me patient, Papa; they were so kind. And nobody would have believed it, if I wasn't always cross, you know."

"Not cross now, my little woman," he said smiling.

"Oh! I said I never could be cross again, now Mamma is better; but Miss Fosbrook says I shall sometimes feel so, and I do believe she is right, for I was almost cross to Georgie to-day. But she says one may FEEL cross, and not BE cross!"

He did not quite know all that his little girl was thinking of; but he patted her fondly, and said, "Yes, there is a great deal to be thankful for, my dear; and I shall trust to you elder ones to give your Mamma no trouble while I am afloat."

"I will try," said Bessie. "And please, Papa, would you tell Nurse about it? She doesn't half believe us, and she is so tiresome about Miss Fosbrook!"

"Tiresome! what do you mean?"

"She always thinks what she does is wrong, and she puts nonsense into Johnnie's head, and talks about favourites. Mary told Susan it was jealousy."

The Captain spoke pretty strongly to Nurse Freeman that evening, but it is doubtful if she were the better for it. She was a very good woman in most things, but she could not bear that the children should be under anyone but herself; and just as Henry lost the truth by inaccuracy, she lost it by prejudice.

Miss Fosbrook was glad to get away from the dining-room, where it was rather awful to sit without her work and be talked to by Mr. Merrifield, even though she liked him much better than she had expected.

Charlotte M. Yonge

When David came to bed, she sat by him and talked to him about his angry unforgiving spirit. She could not but think he was in a fearful temper, and she tried hard to make him sorry for his brother, instead of thirsting to see the disappointment visited on him; but David could not see what she meant. Wicked people ought to be punished; it was wicked to steal and tell stories, and he hoped Henry would be punished, so as he would never forget it, for hindering poor Hannah from getting her pig.

He would not understand Henry's predicament; he was only angry, bitterly angry, and watching for vengeance. Miss Fosbrook could not reason or persuade him out of it, nor make him see that he could hardly say his prayers in such a mood. Indeed, he would rather have gone without his prayers than have ceased to hope for Henry's punishment.

Perhaps in this there was sense of justice and indignation against wrong doing, as well as personal resentment. Miss Fosbrook tried to think so, and left him, but not without praying for him, that a Christian temper of forgiveness might be sent upon him.

All the others were subdued and awe-struck. It was not yet known what was to happen to Henry; but there was a notion that it would be very terrible indeed, and that Uncle John would be sure to make it worse; and they wished Miss Fosbrook good-night with very sad faces.

CHAPTER XIV.

Nothing had as yet befallen Henry, for he came down to breakfast in the morning; but his father did not greet him, and spoke no word to him all the time they were in the room together. The children felt that this was indeed terrific. Such a thing had never befallen any of them before. They would much rather have been whipped; and even David's heart sank.

Something, however, was soon said that put all else out of his sisters' minds. The Captain turned to them with his merry smile, saying, "Pray what would Miss Susie and Miss Bessie say to coming up to London with me to see Mamma?"

The two girls bounded upon their chairs; Susan's eyes grew round, and Bessie's long; the one said, "O Papa!" and the other, "Oh, thank you!" and they looked so overwhelmed with ecstasy, and all the three elders laughed.

"Then you will behave discreetly, young women?"

"I'll try," said Susan; "and Bessie always does. Oh, thank you, Papa!"

"Grandmamma should be thanked; she asked me to bring a child or two, to be with Mamma when I go down to Portsmouth. We had thought of Susan; but I think Betty deserves some amends for what she has undergone."

"Oh yes, Papa! thank you!" cried Susan, Sam, and David, from their hearts; John and Annie because the others did so.

"Then you won't kick her out if she shares your berth, Sue?"

"Oh, I am so glad, Papa! It is so nice to go together."

"Then, Miss Fosbrook, will you be kind enough to rig them out? I must drive into Southminster at ten o'clock; and if you would be so good as to see them smartened up for London there, I should be much obliged to you."

The mere drive to the country town was a great event in itself, even without the almost incredible wonder that it was to lead to; and the delights of which Ida and Miss Fosbrook had told them in London went so wildly careering through the little girls' brains, that they hardly knew what they said or did, as they danced about the house, and ran up-stairs to get ready, long before ten o'clock.

Mr. Carey had been informed that his pupils would not come to him during the few days of their father's stay; and Sam begged to ride in on his pony by the side of the carriage; but he was desired to fetch his books, and call Henry, as his uncle wished to give them both an examination. Was this the beginning of captivity to Uncle John? David and Johnnie were quite angry. They considered it highly proper that Hal should be shut up with Uncle John, but they thought it very hard that Sam should be so used too; and Sam himself looked very round-backed, reluctant, and miserable, partly at the task, partly at being deprived of the sight of his father for several hours of one of those few precious days.

Miss Fosbrook wished Susan to have sat on the front seat of the old phaeton with her father; but he would not consent to this, and putting the two little girls together behind, handed the governess to the place of honour beside him, where she felt rather shy, in spite of his bright easy manner.

"I am afraid," he said, after having flourished his whip merrily at Johnnie, Annie, and Davie, who were holding open the iron gate, "that you have had a tough job with those youngsters! We never meant you to have been left so long to their mercy."

"I know - I know; I only wish I could have done better."

"You have done wonders. My brother hardly knows where he is - never saw those children so mannerly."

Miss Fosbrook could not show how delighted she was.

"I could hardly have ventured on taking those two girls to town unless you had broken them in a little. I would say nothing last night till I had watched Susan; for my mother is particular, and if my wife was to be always worrying herself about their manners, they had better be at home."

" Indeed, I think you may quite trust to their behaving

well. Those two and Sam are so thoroughly trust-worthy, that I had no real difficulty till this unhappy business."

The Captain wanted to talk this over with her, and hear her account of it once more. She gave it fully, thinking he ought to know exactly how his children had acted in the matter, and wishing to explain where she thought she had made mistakes. When she had finished, he said, "Thank you," and considered a little while; then said, "A thing like this brings out a great deal of character; and a new eye sometimes sees more what is in a child than those that bred him up."

"It has been a touchstone, indeed," she answered.

"Poor Hal!" he said sadly; then resumed, "I've said nothing of it yet to the boys - but Admiral Penrose has promised to let me take out one with me. I had thought most of Hal; he seemed to me a smarter fellow, more likely to make his way than his brother; but this makes me doubt whether there can be stuff enough in him. I might not be able to look after him, nor do I know what his messmates may be; and I should not choose to risk it, except with a boy I could thoroughly trust."

"Those young Grevilles seem to me Hal's bane and temptation."

"Ay, ay; but if a boy is of the sort, he'll find someone to be his bane, wherever he goes. I'll have no more of the Grevilles though. If he should not go with me, my brother John would take him into his house, and keep a sharp look out after him. Just tell me, if you have no objection, how the boy strikes you. Most people think him the most taking of the lot."

"So he is," said Christabel thoughtfully; "he has more ease and readiness, and he is affectionate and warm-hearted; but then he is a great talker, and fond of boasting."

"Exactly. I told him that was the very way he learnt falsehood."

"I am afraid, too," she was obliged to add, "that his resolutions run away in talk. He has not much perseverance; and he is easily led."

"Well, I believe you are right; but then what's to be done? I can hardly afford to lose this chance; but Sam was always backward; and I doubt his even caring to go to sea."

"Oh! Captain Merrifield!"

"What! has he given you reason to think that he does?" She told him how she had found Sam struggling with his longing for the sea and his father; and how patiently the boy had resigned himself to see his brother put before him, and himself condemned for being too dull and slow.

"Did I say so? I suppose he had put me past my patience with blundering over his lessons. I never meant to make any decision; but I did not think he wished it."

"He said it had been his desire from the time he could remember, especially when he felt the want of you during your last voyage."

"Very odd; how reserved some boys are! I declare I

Charlotte M. Yonge

was vexed that it had gone out of his head; though I thought it might be for the best. You know I was not born to this place. I never dreamt of it till my poor brother Sam's little boy went off in a fever six years ago, and we had to settle down here. Before that, we meant my eldest to follow my own profession; but when he seemed to take to the soil so kindly, I thought, after all, he might make the happier squire for never having learnt the smell of salt water, nor the spirit of enterprise; but if it were done already, the first choice is due to him. You are sure?"

"Ask the girls."

He leant back and shouted out the question, "Sue! do you know whether Sam wishes to go to sea?"

"There's nothing he ever wished so much," was the answer.

"Then why didn't he say so?"

"Because he thought it would be no use," screamed Susan back.

"No use! why?"

"Because Hal says Admiral Penrose promised him. O Papa! are you going to take Sam?"

"Oh dear! we can't get on without him!" sighed Elizabeth.

"Are you sure he would like it?" said her father. "I thought he never cared to hear of the sea."

"He can't bear to talk of it, because it makes him so sorry," said Susan.

"And," cried Bessie, "he burnt his dear little ship, the Victory, because he couldn't bear to look at it after you said THAT, Papa."

"After I said what?"

"That he was not smart enough to learn the ropes."

"Very silly of him," said the Captain, "to take in despair what was only meant to spur him on. I suppose now I shall find he has dawdled so much that he couldn't get through an examination."

This shut up the mouths of both the girls, who were afraid that he might not, since they saw a good deal of his droning habits over his lessons, and heard more of Hal's superior cleverness.

Miss Fosbrook ventured to say, "You may expect a great deal of a boy who works on a pure principle of obedience."

"You think a great deal of that youngster," said the Captain, highly gratified. "It is the first time I ever knew a stranger take to him."

"I did not take to him as a stranger. I thought him uncouth and dull. I only learnt to love and respect him, as I felt how perfectly I might rely on him, and how deep and true his principles are. If the children have gone on tolerably well in your absence, it is because he has always stood by me, and his weight of character has told on them."

Captain Merrifield did not answer at once; he bit his lip, then blew his nose, and cleared his throat, before he said, "Miss Fosbrook, you have made me very happy; it will make his mother so. She always rated him so high, that I half thought it was a weakness for her eldest son; but there! I suppose he was down-hearted about this fancy of his, poor boy; and that hindered him from making the most of himself. I wonder what sort of a figure he is cutting before his uncle!"

The town was at length reached; and the shopping was quite wonderful to the sisters. Miss Fosbrook found a shop where the marvellous woman undertook to send home two grey frocks trimmed with pink, by the next evening; and found two such fashionable black silk jackets, that Susie felt quite ashamed of herself, though rather pleased; and Bessie only wished she could see her own back, it must look so like Ida's. Then there were white sleeves, and white collars, that made them feel like young women; and little pink silk hand-kerchiefs for their necks; and two straw hats, which Miss Fosbrook undertook to trim with puffs of white ribbon, and a pink rosette at each ear. Bessie thought they would be the most beautiful things that had ever been in her possession, and was only dreading that Sam would say they were like those on Ida Greville's donkey's best harness; while Susan looked quite frightened at them, whispered a hope that Mamma would not think them too fine, and that Miss Fosbrook would not let them cost too much money; and when assured that all fell within what Papa had given to be laid out, she begged that Annie and little Sally might have the like.

But as they were not going to London, Miss Fosbrook

could not venture on this; and as Bessie had set her affections upon a certain white chip hat, with a pink border and a white feather, both sisters remained wishing for something - as is sure to happen on such occasions.

However, Elizabeth recovered from the hat when she was out of sight of it; and they went and saw the cathedral, where the painted windows and grave grand arches filled her with a truer and wiser sense of what was beautiful; and then they walked a long time up and down under its buttressed wall, waiting for Papa, till they grew tired and hungry; but at last he came in a great hurry, and sorry to have been hindered. With naval politeness, he gave his arm to Miss Fosbrook, and carried them off to a pastry-cook's, where he bade them eat what they pleased, and spend the rest of the florin he threw them on buns for the little ones, while he fetched the carriage; and so they all drove home again, and found the rest of the party ravenous, having waited dinner for three-quarters of an hour.

Wonderful to relate, Uncle John had not eaten anybody up! not even Baby; though Papa advised Susan to make sure that she was safe, and then sent Sam to ask Purday for a salad. Perhaps this was by way of getting rid of this constant follower while he asked his brother what he thought of the boys' attainments.

Uncle John could not speak very highly of the learning of either; but he said, "Sam knows thoroughly what he does know. As to the other, he thinks he knows everything, and makes most awful shots. When I asked them who Dido's husband was, Sam told me he did not know, and Hal, that he was Diodorus Siculus - AT LEAST, Scipio - no, he meant Sicyon."

Charlotte M. Yonge

"Then you think neither could stand an examination for the cadetship?"

"I could not be sure of Sam; but I am quite sure that Hal could not."

Here the dinner-bell rang; the hungry populace rushed to the dining-room, and the meal was gone through as merrily as could be, while still the father never spoke to Henry. Uncle John was as pleasant and good-natured as possible. Who would have thought of the marked difference he made between dining with barbarians, or young gentlefolks!

Dinner over, Captain Merrifield called Sam, - or rather, since that was not necessary, as Sam was never willingly a yard from his elbow, he ordered the others not to follow as they went into the garden together.

"Sam," he said, "Admiral Penrose is kind enough to offer me a berth in the Ramilies for one of you. If you can pass the examination, should you wish to avail yourself of the offer?"

Sam grew very red in the face, looked down, and twirled the button of his sleeve. He certainly was not a gracious boy, for all he said was in a gruff hoarse voice, without even thanks, "Not if it is for this."

"For this! What do you mean, Sam?" said Captain Merrifield, thinking either that the boy was faint-hearted, or that his wish had been the mere fancy of the girls.

"Not if it is to punish Hal," said Sam, with another effort.

"That is not the question. Do you wish it?"

Sam hung his head, and made his eyebrows come down, as if they were to serve as a veil to those horrid tears in his eyes; and after all, his voice sounded sulky, as he said, "Yes."

"Is that all?" said the Captain, angry and disappointed. "Is that the way you take such an offer? If you had rather stay here, and be bred up to be a country squire, say so at once; don't mince the matter!"

"O Papa!" cried Sam indignantly, "how can you think that? Didn't I always want to be like you?"

"Then why can't you say so?"

"Because I can't bear to cut Hal out!" said Sam, putting his arm over his eyes, as a way he considered secret of disposing of his tears.

"Put that out of your head, Sam; or if you don't fancy the sea, have it out at once."

"O Papa! please listen. You know, though Miss Fosbrook is very jolly, we couldn't help getting nohow when you were away, US two particularly."

"You have no mischief to confess, surely, Sam?" said his father, really imagining that this preference to Hal was acting on him so as to make him mention some concealed misdemeanour; "if you have, you know truth is the best line."

"But I haven't, Papa," said Sam, looking up, quite surprised. "You know I am a year older, and couldn't

Charlotte M. Yonge

help caring more; and Miss Fosbrook is so nice, one couldn't bother her; but you see the Grevilles WOULD put it into Hal's head that it was stupid and like a girl to mind her. It is all their fault; and they were sneaks about the turkey-cock, and wouldn't pay - and I know he would have ended by putting the money back when he could, only Davie made such a row before he could; and he did so reckon on the navy - he would pay it back the first thing." The last sentences came between gasps, very like sobs.

"Have done with Hal," said Captain Merrifield, still with displeasure. "I wouldn't take him now on any account. If the Grevilles lead him wrong, what would he do among the mids? If he acts dishonourably here, we should have him disgracing himself and his profession. Since he can't take it, and you won't, I shall try to make some exchange of the chance till John or David will be old enough."

"But Papa, I - " began Sam.

"*I* don't want to force you to it," continued Captain Merrifield, in his vexed voice. "I never mean to force my sons to any profession if I can help it; and you have a right to be considered. It has always been a disadvantage to me, and to this place, that I was bred to the sea instead of to farming; and though you can't live on the property without some profession, it may be quite as well that you should turn your mind to something else - only if it be the army, I can't help you on in it."

"I had rather go to sea, if you please," said Sam.

"Don't say so to please me," said his father. "I tell you,

the examinations are a pretty deal harder than they were in my time. It is not a trade for a youngster to be idle in; and I won't have you, just when you've knocked about a few years, and are getting fit to be of use on board and nowhere else, calling yourself heartily sick of it, and turning round to say it was my doing."

"I'll never do that, Papa," said poor Sam, unable to understand why his father should speak as though scolding him.

"No? And mind, you must take the rough with the smooth, if you sail with me, and not be always running after me, Papa-ing me. I can't see after you, and should only get you ill will if I tried."

"I had rather go," said Sam.

"I'm sure I don't know what to make of you," said his father, looking at him in a puzzle. "However, if you do mean to go, you may tell Freeman to get your things ready to come up with me on Thursday; only if you don't really like the notion, find out your own mind, and let me know in time, that's all."

The Captain turned away, and gave a long whistle - an accustomed signal - that brought children and dogs all rushing and tumbling about him together, to walk with him about the farm, and his brother among them; but Sam hung back. He had not the heart to go with that merry throng; for he did not know whether his father were not displeased with him, and he therefore thought he must be to blame.

People who, like Sam, rather cultivate the habit of

gruffness and reserve, and prefer to be short and rude, become so utterly unable to express what they mean, that on great occasions they are misunderstood, and give pain by supposed ingratitude and dislike, even when they feel most warmly. Captain Merrifield could only judge from looks and words; and even when Sam had been satisfied about Henry, he had shown so little alacrity or satisfaction, as really to leave a doubt whether he were not unwillingly yielding to his father's wishes; which would have been a mistaken act, as the Captain thought no one ought to be a sailor unless with a very strong desire that way. Thus Sam really perplexed and distressed his father, when he least intended it; and unable to understand what was the matter, yet feeling heavy and sad, he turned aside from the rest, and, by way of the quietest place he could find, climbed up a tall pear-tree, to the very highest branch he could reach. He put himself astride on one bough, his feet upon another below, and his back leaning against the main stem. No one could see him up so high among the thick leaves; but he could see all around the village, and over the house; he could look down into the farm-court at the pigs burying themselves in the straw; and out beyond at the geese and ducks in the meadow, and the broods of chickens pecking and scratching about, or the older poultry rolling in the dust-holes they had scraped for themselves. He could see Purday among his cabbages in the garden; and further off, could watch the walking-party through the fields, his father with little George in his arms, and Uncle John as often as possible by his side; while the others frisked about, sometimes spreading out like a flock of sheep in the pasture land, or when they came to the narrow paths in the cornfields, all getting into single file, and being lost sight of all but their heads.

Sam recollected how, the day when he had heard that he was not likely to be a sailor, he had felt as if he hated Stokesley, and as if it would be a prison to him, and how everything reminding him of the sea had been a misery to him. He would not then have believed anyone who had told him that he would really hear of his appointment and be so little glad. Yet for two whole years the loss of the hope had weighed on him, and made him dull whenever he thought of grown-up life, heard of the sea, or was asked what he was to be: and almost always, at his prayers, he had that meaning in his mind, when he said "Thy Will be done;" he had really submitted patiently, and tried to put away the longing from his mind, and would, there can be no doubt, have been happy and dutiful at home; but at length the wish of his heart was suddenly granted.

And then, wish though it still were, there came all this grief and discomfort. The gladness was in him some-where, but he could not get at it, either for his own comfort, or that of his father. He missed his mother exceedingly. SHE would know what he meant, and tell Papa that he did care to go. Yet, did he care so very much? Only think of beginning to be a stranger at this dear old home! and seeing no mother, no Susie, nor any of them, for years together - probably not his father after the first voyage! However, the sailor was too strong in Sam for that grief not to pass off; and his chief trouble was the sense of supplanting Henry. He knew the disappointment would be most bitter; and he could not get rid of the sense of having taken an unfair advantage of the disgrace of Henry's adventure. As to his father's manner, he got over that more easily, for his conscience was free; he knew that the tone of displeasure would be gone at the next meeting, and he was too sure of his own love of the sea to fear that he should not show it enough. After all, he was to be a naval cadet! He could not be sorry. Nay, he felt he had his wish; the very wish he had thought it wrong to put into a prayer. He thought he ought to be thankful that it was granted, in the same way as he had been when his mother began to recover. So he put his hands together, and looked up into the summer blue sky through the leaves, and his lips moved, as he whispered his thanks, and asked to be helped in being a good brave sailor, and that something as good might happen to poor Henry.

After this, somehow, the weight was gone, he knew not where. All he recollected was, that he should see Mamma in two days, and that he was to sail with Papa if he could get through his examination. There was a sort of necessity of doing something comical; and just then spying Miss Fosbrook with a book walking slowly below, he could not resist the temptation of sending down on her a shower of little hard pears and twigs.

Bob came one down on her book, and another on her bonnet. She looked up, and saw a leg stretching out for a branch, apparently in such a dangerous manner, that she did not know whether she should not have Sam himself on her head next, and started back, watching as he swung himself from branch to branch, and then slid down, embracing the trunk.

"Did I hit you!" said he. "I couldn't help trying it; it was such fun."

It was a great liberty; but she was so good-humoured as to laugh, and said he had taken good aim.

"Please, Miss Fosbrook," next said he, "would you hear how many propositions I can say!" And as she opened her eyes at this holiday amusement, he added, "Papa has got the appointment after all, and means me to have it."

"I am so glad, Sam! I give you joy!" she said, and took his hand to shake it heartily.

"I wish Hal could go too," said Sam.

"Dear Sam," she said kindly, and guessing his feelings, as having gone along with them, "I don't wonder you are sorry for him; but indeed I think it is better for him to be sheltered from beginning real life just now."

"Papa said he would not have taken him," said Sam; "but it seems so hard to have all his life changed for a thing that sounds worse than he meant it to be."

"Sam," said Miss Fosbrook, "I once read a sermon, that said that our conduct in little things does decide the tenor of our lives. You know one moment of hastiness cost Moses the Promised Land; and only a little while ago, we heard how Joash had but few victories allowed to him, because he did not think it worth while to strike the ground as often as Elisha told him. It is the little things that show whether we are to be trusted with great."

"It is such a tremendous punishment," said Sam, "when he would have put it back again."

"My brother knew a banker's clerk who was transported for borrowing what he meant to put back again. No, Sam; people must bear the result of their doings;

and your father judges for Hal as much in kindness as in anger."

"I know he knows best."

"You may see it as well as trust. With all his grand talk, do you really think that Hal would not be upset at the first hardship, or that he could face bullying or danger? Remember the bull, that was at least a vicious cow, and turned out to be a calf."

Sam could not help laughing, as he said, "Yes, that would never do at sea; and he would be done for if he were cowardly there. But I wish I could get out of sight of him till I am gone. And please hear my Euclid; I'll get the book, if you'll stay out here."

"Therefore, if the two sides of two triangles be equal to one another, and the adjacent angles be equal each to each," resounded through the laurels, as the walking party returned.

"Hallo! al fresco Euclid!" exclaimed Uncle John, as Sam with a blush ran after his blotted diagrams, as a sudden gust of wind blew them dancing over the garden. Captain Merrifield caught one, and restored it to Sam, with a pat on the back that made his teeth rattle in his head, but which made him as happy as a young sea-king, showing that they perfectly understood each other.

But to be ever so good a boy does not carry one through the examinations that stand at the door of every road of life for those who are not wealthy. Sam knew he was the dull boy of Mr. Carey's four pupils; and though from sheer diligence he was less often turned back than the rest, yet they could all excel him whenever they chose: his lessons all went against the grain, and were a sore trouble to him; and his uncle had shown much wrath to-day at his ignorance and backwardness. He was therefore in a great fright, and gave himself and Miss Fosbrook no peace, running after her every moment with his Euclid, his Colenso, or his slate.

"That boy will stupefy himself and his admirable cramming machine!" exclaimed Uncle John, when coming out into the court after tea to talk to Purday, the two brothers heard, "The complement A E is equal to the complement D E," proceeding out of the school-room window.

"A truce with your complements to-night," shouted the Captain; "come down, Sam; I must have a game at hide-and-seek!"

Though hide-and-seek on the lawn with Papa was the supremest bliss that life had yet offered to the young Merrifields, and though Susan, Bessie, Annie, and Johnnie, had all severally burst into the room to proclaim it and summon Sam, he had refused them all; but this call settled it; he broke off in the middle of his rectangle, and dashed down stairs, to the great relief of kind Miss Fosbrook, who, with all her good-will, found her head beginning to grow weary of angles and right-angles on a hot evening in the height of summer.

The summer-house was to be HOME, and there the party were assembled - nine in number, for not only Papa, but Uncle John, was going to play; and Henry, though forlorn and unnoticed, had wandered about with the rest all day, trying to do as usual, to forget the

Charlotte M. Yonge

heavy load that pressed on him, and to believe that he was not going to be punished for mere unluckiness in borrowing, and for not answering impertinent questions. The world was very unlike itself to him; and he saw the enjoyment without being able to enter into it, just as a sick person sees the sunshine without feeling the warmth; but instead of penitence, he merely tried to shake off his compunction.

So there he stood in the ring, as Susan was finding out who was to be the first to hide, by pointing to each, at each word of the formula,

> "Eggs, butter, cheese, bread,
> Sticks, stocks, stones, dead."

"Dead" came to Uncle John, as perhaps Susan had contrived; and shrugging up his shoulders, he went off to hide, and his whoop was presently heard. He was not VERY good game; maybe he did not wish to be very long sought, for he was no further than in the tall French beans, generally considered as a stupid place to hide in. The children had been in hopes that he would catch Papa, which was always a very difficult matter, for the sailor was lighter of foot, as well as, of course, longer in limb, than any of the children; but they saw that Uncle John had not the slightest chance with him, and it was Bessie who was caught in her homeward race.

Bessie was rather a good hider, and was searched for far and wide before Sam's "I spy! I spy!" gave the signal that a bit of the spotty cotton had been seen peeping out from under Purday's big potato-basket in the tool-house, and the whole party flew towards home. Bessie would not aim at Papa, for if so, she would certainly catch no one; but she hunted down David, who was too sturdy to be a quick runner, and who was very well pleased to be caught.

"I'll have Papa!" he said, as she captured him. "I know of such a cunning place."

David's place proved to be in among his likenesses, the cabbages, immediately in front of the summer-house. There he lay flat on the very wet mould, among the stout cabbages, all of which had a bead of wet in every wrinkle of their great leaves, so that when Susan had at length spied him, and he came plunging out, his brown-holland - to say nothing of his knees - was in a state that would have caused most mammas to send him to be instantly undressed; but nobody even saw it, and he charged instantly towards the door of the summer-house, not pursuing anyone in particular, but cutting all off from their retreat. He slipped aside, however, and let all the lesser game pass by uncaught; his soul soared higher than even Uncle John, who looked on exceedingly amused at the small man's stratagem, and at the long dodging that took place between him and his father, the quick lithe Captain skipping hither and thither, and trying to pop in one side while his enemy was on the other; and the square, determined, little, puffing, panting boy, guarding his door, hands on knees, ever ready for a dart wherever the attempt was made. The whole party in the home nearly went into fits at the fun, and at the droll remarks Uncle John made at this hare and tortoise spectacle; till at last either the Captain gave in, or Davie made a cleverer attack than ever, for with a great shout he flew upon Papa, and held him fast by the legs. Everyone shrieked with delight; Papa hid in such clever places, and when found, he roared so splendidly, that it struck the little ones with terror, and did the hearts of the elders good, to hear him; indeed, the greatest ambition Johnnie entertained was to roar like Papa. Then he could make his voice sound as if out of any place he chose, so that no one could guess by his "whoop" where to look for him; and this time it seemed to be quite out at the other end of the kitchen-garden, where they were all looking, when another "whoop" came apparently down from Sam's pear-tree on the lawn; and while they were peeping up into it, "whoop" re-echoed from the stables! At last, as Annie was gazing up and round as if she even thought it as well to look right into the sky for Papa, she suddenly beheld the two merriest eyes in the world, on the roof of the summer-house itself. He had been lying there on the thatch, watching at his ease all the wanderings of the seekers, and uttering those wonderful whoops to bewilder them.

"I spy! I spy!" shrieked Annie, flying in, even while her father sprang to the ground, and with Davie's manoeuvre on a larger scale, seemed to be taking his choice of all the fugitives rushing up from all parts.

One elder boy, and one younger, he was hunting down the gooseberry-path, when just as he was about to pounce on the former, he said that it was not Sam, stood still, and folded his arms. A shriek made him look round; little David stood sobbing and crying piteously.

"Davie! what, Davie! What is it, my man? Where are you hurt!"

"No, no! I'm not hurt! Catch Hal, Papa."

"No, David. I do not play with boys that act

like Henry."

"Speak to him, Papa; oh, speak!"

"I shall, before I go," said the Captain gravely.

"Now, now! Papa. Oh, do! I did want him to be punished, but not like this."

"No, David. If he can expect to play with me, and be treated like the others, he is not in the state to receive forgiveness. There, have done crying; let us go on with the game."

But David could not go on playing; he was too unhappy. Not to be forgiven, even if punished, seemed to him too dreadful to happen to anyone; and he thought that he had brought it all on Henry by his letter of accusation. Tardily and dolefully he crept into the house; and Miss Fosbrook met him, looking so woebegone, that she too thought he had hurt himself. She took him, dirt and all, on her lap; and there he sobbed out that Papa wouldn't speak to Hal, and it was very dreadful; and he wished there were no such things as pigs, or money, or secrets; they only made people miserable!

"Dear Davie, they only make people miserable when they care too much about them. Papa will forgive Hal before he goes away, I am sure; only he is making him sorry first, that he may never do such a thing again."

"I don't like it." And David cried sadly, perhaps because partly he was tired with having been on his legs more than usual that day; but his good and loving little self was come home again. He at least had forgiven his brother the wrong done to himself; and there was no hanging back that night from the fulness of prayer; no, he rather felt that he had been unkind; and the last thing heard of him that night was, that as Sam and Hal were coming up-stairs to bed, a little white figure stood on the top of the stairs, and a small voice said, "Hal, please kiss me! I am so sorry I told Papa about -"

"There, hold your tongue," said Hal, cutting him short with the desired kiss, "if you hadn't told, someone else would."

But long after Sam was asleep, Hal was wetting his pillow through with tears.

CHAPTER XV.

Still the silence lasted. Henry had tried at first to persuade himself that it was only by chance that he never heard his own name from lips that used to call it more often than any other. Indeed, he was so much used to favour, that it needed all the awe-struck pity of the rest to prove to him its withdrawal; and he was so much in the habit of thrusting himself before Samuel, that even the sight and sound of the First Book of Euclid, all day long, failed to convince him that his brother could be preferred; above all, as Nurse Freeman had been collecting his clean shirts as well as Sam's, and all the portmanteaus and trunks in the house had been hunted out of the roof. Once, either the spirit of imitation, or his usual desire of showing himself off, made him break in when Sam was knitting his brows frightfully over a sum in proportion. Hal could do it in no time!

So he did; but he put the third term first, and multiplied the hours into the minutes, instead of reducing them to the same denomination; so that he made out that twenty-five men would take longer to cut a field of grass than three, and then could not see that he was wrong; but Miss Fosbrook and Sam both looked so much grieved for him, that a start of fright went through him.

Charlotte M. Yonge

Some minds really do not understand a fault till they see it severely visited; and "at least" and "couldn't help" had so blinded Henry's eyes that he had thought himself more unlucky than to blame, till his father's manner forced it on him that he had done something dreadful. Vaguely afraid, he hung about, looking so wretched that he was a piteous sight; and it cut his father to the heart to spend such a last day together. Mayhap the Captain could hardly have held out all that second day, if he had not passed his word to his brother.

The travellers were to set off at six in the morning, to meet the earliest train: and it was not till nine o'clock at night, when the four elder ones said good-night, that the Captain, following them out of the room, laid his hand on Henry as the others went up-stairs, and said, "Henry, have you nothing to say to me?"

Henry leant against the baluster and sobbed, not knowing what else to do.

"You can't be more grieved than I am to have such a last day together," said his father, laying his hand on the yellow head; "but I can't help it, you see. If you will do such things, it is my duty to make you repent of them."

Hal threw himself almost double over the rail, and something was heard about "sorry," and "never."

"Poor little lad!" said his father aloud to himself; "he is cut up enough now; but how am I to know if his sorrow is good for anything?"

"O Papa! I'll never do such a thing again!"

"I wish I knew that, Hal," said the Captain, sitting down on the stairs, and taking him between his knees. "There, let us talk it over together. I don't suppose you expected to steal and deceive when you got up in the morning."

"Oh no, no!"

"Go back to the beginning. See how you came to this."

As he waited for an answer, Hal mumbled out after some time, "You said we need not go to church on a week-day."

"Well, what of that?"

"I didn't go in case the telegraph should come."

"There are different ways of thinking," said his father. "Church was the only place where I COULD have gone that St. Barnabas' Day."

"I would have gone," said the self-contradictory Henry, "only the Grevilles are always at one for being like a girl."

"Ha! now we see daylight!" said the Captain.

"'The Grevilles are at one,' - that's more like getting to the bottom of it."

"Yes, Papa," said Hal, glad to make himself out a victim to circumstance; "you can't think what a pair of fellows those are for not letting one alone; Purday says they haven't as much conscience between them as a pigeon's egg has meat; and going down to Mr. Carey's with them every day, they let one have no peace."

"You will find people everywhere who will let you have no peace, unless you do not care for them; though you will not be left to the Grevilles any longer."

"Yes, Papa; when I am away from them, you will see -"

"No, Hal, I shall not see, I shall hear."

"Shall not I sail with you, then, Papa?"

"You will not sail at all: I thought you knew that."

"I thought the Admiral must have given you two appointments," said Hal timidly.

"He gave me ONE, for one of my sons. The first choice is Sam's right, even if he had not deserved it by his brave patient obedience."

Hal hung his head; then said, "But, Papa, if Sam broke down in his examination, please mightn't I -"

"No, Henry. Not only does your uncle say that though Sam's success is very doubtful, your inaccuracy would make your failure certain; but if your knowledge were ever so well up to the mark, I could not put you into the navy. Left to yourself here, you have been insubordinate, vain, weak, shuffling: can I let you go into greater temptation, where disgrace would be public and without remedy?"

"Oh, but, Papa! Papa! Away from the Grevilles, and not under only a governess -"

"You shall be away from the Grevilles, and not under a governess. Your uncle is kind enough to take you with him to his house, and will endeavour to make you fit to try to get upon the foundation by the time there is a vacancy."

"O Papa! don't," sobbed Henry.

"I can't help it, Hal! You have shown yourself unfit either for the sea or for home. What can I do with you?"

"Try me - only try me, Papa. I would -"

"I cannot go by what you say you would be, but what you are. Deeds, not words."

"But if you won't let me go into the navy, only let me be in real school."

"No, Henry; I have not the means of sending you there: excepting on the foundation; and if you get admittance there at all, it will only be by great diligence, and your uncle's kindness in preparing you."

Henry cried bitterly. It was a dreadful prospect to do his lessons alone with Uncle John in the boys' play-hours, and be kept in order by Aunt Alice when his uncle was in school. Perhaps his father would not have liked it himself, for his voice was very pitying, though cheering, as he said, "One half year, Hal, very likely no more if you take pains, and you'll get into school, and be very happy, so long as you don't make a Greville of every idle chap you meet."

Henry cried as though beyond consolation.

"I hate leaving you this way," continued his father; "but by the time I come home you will see it was the best thing for you; and look up to Uncle John as your best friend. Why, Hal, boy, you'll be a tall fellow of fourteen! Let me find you godly and manly: you can't be one without the other. There now, good night, God bless you."

More might have been said to Henry on his fault and what had led to it; but what his father did say was likely to sink deeper as he grew older, and had more sense and feeling.

From him Captain Merrifield went to the school-room, where Miss Fosbrook was packing up for the little girls, and putting last stitches to their equipments, with hearty good-will and kindness, as if she had been their elder sister.

He thanked her most warmly; and without sending away the girls, who were both busy tacking in little white tuckers to the evening frocks, he began to settle about the terms on which she was to remain at Stokesley. He said that he could not possibly have left his wife without a person on whose friendly help and good management of the children he could depend. Important as it was to him to be employed, he must have refused the appointment if Miss Fosbrook had been discontented, or had not had the children so well in hand. He explained that he had reason to think that Mrs. Merrifield's present illness had been the effect of all she had gone through while he was in the Black Sea during the Crimean War. She had been a very strong person, and had never thought of sparing herself; but she and all her little children had had to get into Stokesley in his absence; she had to manage the estate and farm, teach the elder children, and take care of the babies, with no help but Nurse Freeman's: and though he had been wounded when with the Naval Brigade, and had been at death's door with cholera, the effects had done him no lasting harm at all; while the over-strain of the anxiety and exertion that she had undergone all alone had so told upon her, that she had never been well since, and he much feared, would never be in perfect health again. He must depend upon Miss Fosbrook for watching over her and saving her, as his little Susie could not yet do; and for letting him know from time to time how she was going on, and whether he ought to give up everything and come home.

He had tears in his eyes as he thanked Christabel for her earnest promise to watch and tend Mrs. Merrifield with a daughter's care; and her heart swelled with strong deep feeling of sorrow and sympathy with these two brave-hearted loving people, doing their duty at all costs so steadily; and she was full of gladness and thankfulness that they could treat her as a true and trusty friend. He walked away, feeling far too much to bear any eye upon him; and Susan was found to be crying quietly, making her thread wet through, and her needle squeak at every stitch, at the sad news that Mamma never was to be quite well, even though assured that she was likely to be much better than she had been for months past.

Bessie shed no tears; but Miss Fosbrook, who had been hindered all day by Sam's Euclid and Colenso, and had sat up till half-past eleven o'clock to make the two Sunday frocks nice enough for the journey, on going into the bed-room to lay them out for the morning, saw a little face raised from the pillow of one of the small

Charlotte M. Yonge

white beds, and found her broad awake. Bessie never could go to sleep properly when anything out of the common way was coming to pass, so that was the less wonder; but she had a great deal in her head, and she was glad to get Christabel to kneel down by her, to listen to her whispers.

"Dear Christabel, I am so sorry. I never cared about it before!"

"About what, my dear?"

"What Papa said about when he was in the Black Sea. I never knew Mamma cared so much."

"I dare say not, my dear; you were much younger then."

"And I didn't know all about it," said Bessie, "or else I've forgotten. I have been trying to remember whether we ever thought about Mamma; and oh, Christabel! do you know - I believe we only thought she was cross! Oh dear! it was so naughty and bad of us!"

"I can guess how it happened, my dear. You were not old enough to be made her friends, and you could not understand quiet sorrow."

"To think we should have said she was cross!"

"That was wrong, because it was disrespectful. You see, my dear, when grown people are in trouble, you young ones can't enter into their feelings, nor always even find out that anything is amiss; and you get vexed at there being a cloud over the house, and call it crossness."

"Grown-up people are sometimes cross, aren't they?" said Bessie. "Nurse is; and I heard Papa say Aunt Alice was."

"We have tempers, certainly," said Miss Fosbrook; "and unless we have conquered them as children, there will be signs of them afterwards; but very few people, and certainly no children, can tell when grave looks, or words sharper than usual, come from illness or anxiety or sorrow; and it is the only way to save great grief and self-reproach to give one's own faults the blame, and try to be as unobtrusive and obliging as possible."

"And I am older now, and can understand," said Bessie; "but then, it is Susie that is right hand, and does everything."

"There's plenty in your own line, Bessie - plenty of little kindly services that are very cheering; and above all -"

"What?"

"Attending to your Mamma's troubles will drive away your own grievances. Only I will not talk to you any more now, for I want you to go to sleep; if you lie awake, you will be tired to-morrow, and that will incline you to be fretful."

"Fretful to-morrow!"

Bessie could not believe it possible; and indeed Miss Fosbrook did not think the chance great, as long as there was amusement and excitement. The danger would be in the waitings and disappointments that will often occur, even in the height of enjoyable schemes.

Charlotte M. Yonge

It would take too long to tell of all the good-byes. The children old enough to enter into the parting were setting off too; and Miss Fosbrook felt more for the little ones than they did for themselves, as they watched their father and uncle and two sisters into the gig, and the boys into the cart, with Purday to drive them and the boxes, Sam sitting on his father's old midshipman's chest, trying, as well as the jolting would let him, to con over that troublesome Thirty-fifth Proposition, which nine times repetition to Miss Fosbrook had failed to put into his head.

Johnnie and Annie wished themselves going to sea, or to London, or anywhere, rather than having the full force of Miss Fosbrook on their lessons! She did not make them do more, but she took the opportunity of making everything be done thoroughly, and, as they thought, bothered them frightfully about pronouncing their words in reading, and holding their pens when they wrote. After a little while, however, they found that really their hands were much less tired, and their lines much smoother and more slanting, than when they crooked their fingers close down over the ink. Absolutely they began to know the pleasure of doing something well, and they felt so comfortable, that they were wonderfully good; and the pig fund might have had a chance, but David did not seem to think of reviving it. Perhaps his great vehemence had tired itself out; and maybe he was ashamed of the great disturbance he had made and all that had come upon Henry, and did not wish to think of it again, for St. Katherine's fair-day passed over without a word of the pig.

The young ladies were not great letter-writers; and all that was known of them was that Mamma was better, they had been to the Zoological Gardens and the hyena was so funny, and Mrs. Penrose was so nice. Then that Papa and Sam were gone to Portsmouth, and that they had telegraphed that Sam had succeeded.

If it had been her own brother, Miss Fosbrook could not have been much happier; and in honour of it she and the three children all went to drink tea in the wilderness, walking in procession, each with a flag in hand, painted by her for the occasion.

Three days after, when the post came in, there was a letter directed to Master David Douglas Merrifield, Stokesley House, Bonchamp. It was a great wonder; for David was not baby enough, nor near enough to the youngest, to get letters as a pet, nor was he old enough to be written to like an elder one. He spelt the address all over before he made up his mind to open it, and then exclaimed, "But it is not a letter! It's green!"

"It is a post-office order, Davie," said Miss Fosbrook. "Let me look. Yes, for ten shillings. Write your name there; and if we take it to the post-office at Bonchamp, they will give you ten shillings."

"Ten shillings! Oh, Davie!" cried Johnnie, "I wish it was to me!"

"It just makes up for what Hal took, and more too," said Annie. "Where can it come from, Davie?"

"From the Queen," said Davie composedly; "the Queen always does justice."

Miss Fosbrook was quite sorry to confess, for truth's sake, that she did not think the Queen could have heard

Charlotte M. Yonge

of the loss of the pig fund, and that it was more likely to be from someone who wished to make up for the disaster - who could it be? She looked at the round stamp upon the green-lettered paper, and read "Portsmouth." Could it be from Papa? Then she looked at the cover; but it was not a bit like the Captain's writing; it was pretty, lady-like, clear-looking hand-writing, and puzzled her a great deal more. If the children had once had a secret of their own, there was a very considerable one to puzzle them now; and they could hardly believe that Miss Fosbrook knew nothing about it, any more than themselves.

So restless and puzzled were they, that she thought they would never be able to settle quietly to their lessons, and that it would save idleness if she walked with them at once to Bonchamp to get the money. It was two miles; but all three were stout walkers, and they were delighted to go; indeed, they would have fancied that someone else might run away with the ten shillings if they had not made haste to secure it. So "David Douglas Merrifield" was written, with much difficulty to make it small enough, in the very best and roundest hand. The boys were put into clean blouses, Annie's striped cotton came to light; and off set the party through the lanes, each with sixpence in their hand, for it was poor fun to go to Bonchamp, unless one had something to spend there. David wanted a knife, Johnnie wanted a whip, Annie nothing in particular, only to go into a shop, and buy - she didn't know what.

But the wonderful affair at the post-office must have the first turn; and very grand did David feel as the clerk peeped out from his little hole, and looked amused and gracious as the little boy stood on tiptoe to give in his green paper.

"Will you have it in gold or silver, Sir?" he asked.

"In gold, please," said David.

It was something to have a bit of gold in one's possession for the first time in one's life; and David felt as if he had grown an inch taller, and were as good as six years old, as he walked away with the half sovereign squeezed into his hot little palm.

The toy-shop was at the end of the street, and in they went; Johnnie to try all the whistles in the handles of the whips, and be much disgusted that all that had a real sound lash cost a shilling; David to open and shut the sixpenny knives with the gravity of a judge examining their blades; and Annie to gape about, and ask the price of everything, after the tiresome fashion of people, old or young, when they come out bent on spending, but without any aim or object. However, Annie was kind, if she were silly, and she was very fond of Johnnie; so it ended, after a little whispering, in her sixpence being added to his, to buy a real good whip, such as would crack, and not come to pieces.

Just then, what should the children espy, but a nice firm deal box, containing a little saw, a little plane, a hammer, a gimlet, a chisel, and sundry different sizes of nails. Was there ever anything so delightful, especially to David, who loved nothing so well as running after George Bowles the carpenter, and handling his tools. What was the price of them?

Just ten shillings and sixpence. They were very cheap, the woman of the toy-shop said. They had been ordered by an old lady at her grandson's entreaty; but afterwards a misgiving had seized her that the young gentleman would cut his fingers, and she would not take them.

"Miss Fosbrook," whispered David, "may I give back the knife? then I could buy it."

"You have bought and paid for it," said Christabel.

"Somebody else will buy the box," said David wistfully.

Miss Fosbrook, within herself, thought this unlikely, for nobody went to Bonchamp for costly shopping; and she saw that the woman would gladly have had the knife back, if she could have sold the tool-box, which, even at this reduced price, was much too dear for the little boys who frequented the shop.

"Come away now, my dear," she said decidedly. "No, another time, thank you."

David was as nearly crying as ever he was, as he was forced to follow her out of the shop. Those tools were so charming; his fingers tingled to be hammering, sawing, boring holes. Had he lost the chance for that poor blunt knife? Must he wait a whole fortnight for another sixpence, and find the delicious tool-chest gone?

"Dear Davie, I am very sorry," said Christabel when they were in the street.

"That nasty knife!" cried David.

"It is not the knife, Davie," said she; "but that I want to think - I want you to think - why these ten shillings must have been sent."

"Because we lost the money for the pig," said David. "But Kattern Hill fair is over, and I don't want a pig now; I do want the gimlet to make holes -"

"Yes, David; but you know what was saved for the pig came from all of you; you would have had no right to spend it on anything else, unless they all had consented."

"This is my very own," said David; "it was sent to me - myself - me."

"So it seems now; but just suppose you were to have a letter to say that someone - poor Hal himself, perhaps - or Papa - had sent ten shillings to make up the money for the pig, and directed it to you because you cared so much, would it not be a shame to have spent the money upon yourself?"

"Then they should not have sent it without saying," said David.

Miss Fosbrook thought the same, when she saw how hard the trial was to the little boy; but she hoped she was taking the kindest course, as she said, "Now, David, in nine days time, if you are good, you will have had another sixpence. I see no chance of the tools being sold; or if they are, I could send for such a box from London. By that time, perhaps, something will have happened to show who sent the money, and why."

Charlotte M. Yonge

"And if it is all for myself, I may have the tools!" cried David.

"You shall have them, if you really think it is right, when Monday week comes."

CHAPTER XVI.

Ideas were slow in both entering or dying out of David's mind; but while there they reigned supreme. Carpentry had come in as the pig had gone out, and with the more force, because a new window was being put into Mamma's room; and George Bowles was there, with all his delightful tools, letting the little boys amuse themselves therewith, till they had hardly three sound fingers between them; and Nurse Freeman, when she dressed their wounds, could not think what was the use of a lady if she could not keep the children from hurting themselves; but Miss Fosbrook thought that it was better that boys should get a few cuts and bruises than that they should be timid and unhandy.

One evening, all the party walked to carry to Hannah Higgins's little girl a pinafore that Annie had been making. She was a nice, tidy woman, but there was little furniture in her house, and she looked very poor. The garden was large, and in pretty good order; and there was an empty pig-sty, into which Annie peeped significantly.

"No, Miss Annie, we haven't no pig," said Mrs. Higgins. "Ben says, says he, 'Mother, when I'm taken on for carter boy, see if I don't get you a nice little pig, as will eat the garden stuff, and pay the rent.'

"Oh, but -" began Annie, and there she came to a sudden stop.

"Is he likely soon to be a carter boy?" asked Miss Fosbrook.

"No, Ma'am; he is but ten years old, and they don't often take them on under twelve; but he is a good boy to his mother, and a terrible one for leasing."

Miss Fosbrook was obliged to have it explained to her that "leasing" meant gleaning; and she saw the grand pile of small neat bundles of wheat put out to dry on the sunny side of the house.

"O Davie!" cried Annie, as soon as they were outside the gate, "sha'n't we get the pig for Hannah?"

"It is my money, not yours; I shall do what I please with it," said David, rather crossly.

Miss Fosbrook pulled Annie back, and desired her to let David alone; herself wondering what would be the effect of what he had seen.

He had been eager to do good to Hannah when no desire of his own stood in the way; but a formed wish had arisen in his mind, and he loved himself better than Hannah. Christabel dreaded the clearing-up of the secret of the post-office order, lest he should be proved to love himself more than right and justice.

There were not many letters from the absent pair of sisters; they seemed to be much too busy and happy to write, and appeared to be "seeing everything," and to be only just able to put down the names of the wonders. The chief of all, however, was that kind Mrs. Penrose had actually taken them to Portsmouth for a couple of nights, to see the Ramilies, in which she was going to remain till it sailed. They had sat in the Admiral's cabin, and had slept upon "dear little sofas," where they wished they always slept; they had been in Papa's cabin, which was half filled up with a great gun, that can only be fired out at the window (scratched out, and "port-hole" put in.)

"Oh, how delightful! I wish I had a big gun in my room!" cried Johnnie.

And they had seen Sam's chest; and Sam did look so nice in his uniform; and he had dined with them every day. They had dined late, with the grown-up people; and the Admiral was so kind, only rather funny.

Annie wished she were as old as Bessie, as much as John wished to have a gun filling up his whole bed-room.

The next day, their Papa had taken them into the country to see Lady Seabury, Bessie's godmother, a very old lady indeed, older than Grandmamma, and who could not move out of her chair. "She gave me - "wrote Bessie. There again something had been scratched out, and "a kiss" written overhead.

That something was quite a long word, but it had been very completely blotted out; not like the "window," which had only a couple of cross bars, through which it could be plainly read; but there had plainly been first an attempt at smearing it out with the finger, and that not succeeding, an immense shiny black mess, like the black shade of a chafer grub, had been put down on it, and had come off on the opposite side of the sheet.

What could the word be? Annie and David were both sure they could read the lines through all the blot. The first letter was certainly S.

"But," said Miss Fosbrook, "do you think it is quite honourable to try to read what Bessie did not mean us to see?"

They did not quite enter into this, but they left off trying.

"Mamma had been out in the carriage several times; and they were all coming home on Saturday week" - that was the best news of all - "and then we have a secret too for Miss Fosbrook."

David said he was tired of secrets, and would not guess. Annie guessed a great deal; but Miss Fosbrook thought more about the word she would not try to read. She began to have a strong suspicion from whom the post-office order had come, and was the more uneasy about the spending of David's half sovereign; but she durst say nothing, for she knew it could do no good if he felt himself compelled against his own will; and she saw that he was full of thought.

One day the lawn had been mown, and the children where all very busy wheeling their little barrows, and loading them with the short grass; David was with them at first, but when Purday left off work, he marched after the old man in his grave deliberate way, and was seen no more till nearly tea-time, when he walked into the school-room with a very set look upon his solemn face, and sat himself down cross-legged on the locker, with a sigh that seemed to come out of the very depths of his heart.

"What's the matter, David?"

He made no answer, and Miss Fosbrook let him alone; but Annie presently bounced in, crying out, "Davie, Davie! where were you? We have been hunting for you everywhere! Where did you go?"

"I went with Purday."

"What, to milk the cows?"

"Yes."

"And then?"

"I went with him to Farmer Long's, to see his little Chinese pigs."

"And you have bought one! O Davie!"

"Purday is to ask the farmer about the price to-morrow morning, because he wasn't at home."

"Then you won't get the carpenter's tools?" said Annie.

"No," said David; "Purday said tools that they make for little boys never will cut."

"So you told Purday all about it?"

David nodded his head.

"Oh, do tell me what Purday said!" continued Annie.

"It's nothing to you," said David bluntly. But by and by, when John came in, and a few more questions were asked, David let out that Purday had said, "Well, he thought sure enough if the money was sent to Master David for that intent, he did not ought to spend it no other ways; and whether or not, Hannah Higgins was a deserving woman; and Master Davie didn't know what it was like never to have a bit of bacon ne'er a Sunday in the winter. He couldn't say but it was hard that those poor folks should get nothing but bread and cabbages from week's end to week's end, just that Master Davie might spoil bits of deal board with making chips of them."

And when David was sure he shouldn't spoil his wood, Purday had told him that them toy-shop young gentleman's tools were made to sell, and not made to cut. Best save up his money, and buy one real man's tool after another; and then he'd get a set equal to George Bowles's in time!

Though so young, David was long-sighted and patient enough to see the sense of this, and had already made up his mind that he would begin with a gimlet. And though he did not say so, and the first resolution had cost a very tough struggle, his heart seemed to have freed itself in that one great sigh, and he was at peace with himself.

Miss Fosbrook was very glad he had gone to so wise and good an adviser as Purday, and was almost as happy as David himself. She gave him and John leave to go with Purday the next day to bargain for the pig, as David was very anxious for one in especial, whose face he said was so jolly fat; and it was grand to see the two little boys consequentially walking on either aide of Purday, who had put on his whitest round frock for the great occasion.

Farmer Long was at home; he came out and did the honours of his ten little pigs; and when he found which was David's favourite, he declared that it was the best of the lot, and laughed till David blushed, at the young gentleman's having got such an eye for a pig. "It was a regular little Trudgeon," said Purday, (meaning perhaps a Trojan;) and it was worth at least twelve shillings, but the farmer in his good-nature declared that little Master should have it for the ten, as it was for a present. Hannah's boy was working for him, and was a right good lad, and he would give him some straw for the pig's bed when he went home at night. Then he took the two boys into the parlour, and while Purday had a glass of beer in the kitchen, Mrs. Long gave each of them a big slice of plum-cake, and wanted very much to have given them some wine, but that they knew they must not have; and she inquired after their Mamma and Papa, and made them so much of visitors, that David was terribly shy, and very glad when it was over, though John liked it, and talked fast.

As to the giving the pig, that was a serious business; and David felt hot and shy, and wanted to get it over as soon as possible without a fuss.

So he bolted into Mrs. Higgins's cottage, put his hands behind his back, and spoke thus:- "Please, Mrs. Higgins, put your pig-sty in order! We've all done it - at least they all wanted to - and a green order came down in a letter - and we've bought the pig, and Ben will drive it home when he comes from work!"

And then, as if he had been in a great fright, he ran

Charlotte M. Yonge

away; while Johnnie stayed, and, when Hannah understood, received so many curtsies, and listened to so much pleasure, that he could hardly think of anything else, and felt very glad that SOME pence of his had been in Toby Fillpot.

Annie said that it was not fair that she had not been at the giving the pig; and Miss Fosbrook was a little disappointed too; but then it was much better that David should not want to make a display, so she would not complain, and comforted Annie by putting her in mind that they could go and see the little pig in his new quarters.

A few days more, and the carriage was driving up to the door with dear Mamma in it, and - why, there were three little girls, not two! One look, and the colour came into Christabel's face. It was her youngest little sister, Dora, who sat beside Bessie! Mrs. Merrifield had gone to see Mrs. Fosbrook, and ask if she could take anything for her to her daughter; and she had been so much shocked at the sight of the little pale London faces, that she had begged leave to take home one of the children to spend a month with her sister at Stokesley, since Miss Fosbrook could not be spared to go home at present. Was not that a secret for Christabel? How these two sisters did hug each other!

But the Stokesley secrets have lasted long enough; and there is no time to tell of the happy days of Dora's visit, and the good care that Johnnie took of her whenever she went out, and of her pretty quiet ways that made Bessie take her for her dearest of friends. And still less can be told of the smooth, peaceful, free spirit that seemed to have come home with Mamma, even though she was still able to do little among the children, for the very having her in the house appeared to keep things from going wrong.

One thing must be told, however, and that is, that when Annie told all the wonderful story of the post-office order and the Chinese pig, Bessie grew redder and redder in the face, and Susan squeezed both her hands tight together, and said "May I tell, Bessie!"

Charlotte M. Yonge

Choose from Thousands of 1stWorldLibrary Classics By

Adolphus WilliamWard
Aesop
Agatha Christie
Alexander Aaronsohn
Alexander Kielland
Alexandre Dumas
Alfred Gatty
Alfred Ollivant
Alice Duer Miller
Alice Turner Curtis
Alice Dunbar
Ambrose Bierce
Amelia E. Barr
Andrew Lang
Andrew McFarland Davis
Anna Sewell
Annie Besant
Annie Hamilton Donnell
Annie Payson Call
Anton Chekhov
Arnold Bennett
Arthur Conan Doyle
Arthur Ransome
Atticus
B. M. Bower
Basil King
Bayard Taylor
Ben Macomber
Booth Tarkington
Bram Stoker
C. Collodi
C. E. Orr
C. M. Ingleby
Carolyn Wells
Catherine Parr Traill
Charles A. Eastman
Charles Dickens
Charles Dudley Warner
Charles Farrar Browne
Charles Ives
Charles Kingsley
Charles Lathrop Pack
Charles Whibley
Charles Willing Beale
Charlotte M. Braeme
Charlotte M.Yonge
Clair W. Hayes
Clarence Day Jr.
Clarence E. Mulford

Clemence Housman
Confucius
Cornelis DeWitt Wilcox
Cyril Burleigh
D. H. Lawrence
Daniel Defoe
David Garnett
Don Carlos Janes
Donald Keyhole
Dorothy Kilner
Dougan Clark
E. Nesbit
E.P.Roe
E. Phillips Oppenheim
Edgar Allan Poe
Edgar Rice Burroughs
Edith Wharton
Edward J. O'Biren
John Cournos
Edwin L. Arnold
Eleanor Atkins
Elizabeth Cleghorn
Gaskell
Elizabeth Von Arnim
Ellem Key
Emily Dickinson
Erasmus W. Jones
Ernie Howard Pie
Ethel Turner
Ethel Watts Mumford
Eugenie Foa
Eugene Wood
Evelyn Everett-Green
Everard Cotes
F. J. Cross
Federick Austin Ogg
Ferdinand Ossendowski
Francis Bacon
Francis Darwin
Frances Hodgson Burnett
Frank Gee Patchin
Frank Harris
Frank Jewett Mather
Frank L. Packard
Frederick Trevor Hill
Frederick Winslow Taylor
Friedrich Kerst
Friedrich Nietzsche
Fyodor Dostoyevsky

Gabrielle E. Jackson
Garrett P. Serviss
Gaston Leroux
George Ade
Geroge Bernard Shaw
George Ebers
George Eliot
George MacDonald
George Orwell
George Tucker
George W. Cable
George Wharton James
Gertrude Atherton
Grace E. King
Grant Allen
Guillermo A. Sherwell
Gulielma Zollinger
Gustav Flaubert
H. A. Cody
H. B. Irving
H. G. Wells
H. H. Munro
H. Irving Hancock
H. Rider Haggard
H. W. C. Davis
Hamilton Wright Mabie
Hans Christian Andersen
Harold Avery
Harold McGrath
Harriet Beecher Stowe
Harry Houidini
Helent Hunt Jackson
Helen Nicolay
Hendy David Thoreau
Henrik Ibsen
Henry Adams
Henry Ford
Henry Frost
Henry James
Henry Jones Ford
Henry Seton Merriman
Henry Wadsworth
Longfellow
Henry W Longfellow
Herbert A. Giles
Herbert N. Casson
Herman Hesse
Homer
Honore De Balzac

Horace Walpole
Horatio Alger, Jr.
Howard Pyle
Howard R. Garis
Hugh Lofting
Hugh Walpole
Humphry Ward
Ian Maclaren
Israel Abrahams
J.G.Austin
J. Henri Fabre
J. M. Barrie
J. Macdonald Oxley
J. S. Knowles
J. Storer Clouston
Jack London
Jacob Abbott
James Allen
James Lane Allen
James Andrews
James Baldwin
James DeMille
James Joyce
James Oliver Curwood
James Oppenheim
James Otis
Jane Austen
Jens Peter Jacobsen
Jerome K. Jerome
John Burroughs
John F. Kennedy
John Gay
John Glasworthy
John Habberton
John Joy Bell
John Milton
John Philip Sousa
Jonathan Swift
Joseph Carey
Joseph Conrad
Joseph Jacobs
Julian Hawthrone
Julies Vernes
Justin Huntly McCarthy
Kakuzo Okakura
Kenneth Grahame
Kate Langley Bosher
L. A. Abbot
L. T. Meade
L. Frank Baum
Laura Lee Hope

Laurence Housman
Leo Tolstoy
Leonid Andreyev
Lewis Carroll
Lilian Bell
Lloyd Osbourne
Louis Tracy
Louisa May Alcott
Lucy Fitch Perkins
Lucy Maud Montgomery
Lydia Miller Middleton
Lyndon Orr
M. H. Adams
Margaret E. Sangster
Margaret Vandercook
Maria Edgeworth
Maria Thompson Daviess
Mariano Azuela
Marion Polk Angellotti
Mark Overton
Mark Twain
Mary Austin
Mary Cole
Mary Rowlandson
Mary Wollstonecraft
Shelley
Max Beerbohm
Myra Kelly
Nathaniel Hawthrone
O. F. Walton
Oscar Wilde
Owen Johnson
P.G.Wodehouse
Paul and Mable Thorn
Paul G. Tomlinson
Paul Severing
Peter B. Kyne
Plato
R. Derby Holmes
R. L. Stevenson
Rabindranath Tagore
Rahul Alvares
Ralph Waldo Emmerson
Rene Descartes
Rex E. Beach
Richard Harding Davis
Richard Jefferies
Robert Barr
Robert Frost
Robert Gordon Anderson
Robert L. Drake

Robert Lansing
Robert Michael Ballantyne
Robert W. Chambers
Rosa Nouchette Carey
Ross Kay
Rudyard Kipling
Samuel B. Allison
Samuel Hopkins Adams
Sarah Bernhardt
Selma Lagerlof
Sherwood Anderson
Sigmund Freud
Standish O'Grady
Stanley Weyman
Stella Benson
Stephen Crane
Stewart Edward White
Stijn Streuvels
Swami Abhedananda
Swami Parmananda
T. S. Ackland
The Princess Der Ling
Thomas A. Janvier
Thomas A Kempis
Thomas Anderton
Thomas Bailey Aldrich
Thomas Bulfinch
Thomas De Quincey
Thomas H. Huxley
Thomas Hardy
Thomas More
Thornton W. Burgess
U. S. Grant
Valentine Williams
Victor Appleton
Virginia Woolf
Walter Scott
Washington Irving
Wilbur Lawton
Wilkie Collins
Willa Cather
Willard F. Baker
William Makepeace
Thackeray
William W. Walter
Winston Churchill
Yei Theodora Ozaki
Young E. Allison
Zane Grey